FROTH
AND
GOBLETS

TED SCOTT

BALBOA.
PRESS
A DIVISION OF HAY HOUSE

Balboa Press books may be ordered through booksellers or by contacting:

Balboa Press
A Division of Hay House
1663 Liberty Drive
Bloomington, IN 47403
www.balboapress.com.au
1-(877) 407-4847

ISBN: 978-1-4525-0500-8 (sc)
ISBN: 978-1-4525-0501-5 (e)

Printed in the United States of America

Balboa Press rev. date: 04/30/2012

PREFACE

"Although you may attempt to do a hundred things in this
world, only Love will give you release from the bondage
of yourself."

Jami

This is a book about depression and its alleviation.

I do not in any way pretend to have discovered a cure for depression
and I don't want to trivialize this ubiquitous and debilitating condition.
The prevalence of depression has greatly increased over recent decades.
It has become a huge problem in many countries. It is a cause that has
been taken on by some of the celebrities in our society and helped by
the fact that many other prominent people have admitted that they have
been its victims.

My work has been informed by the mentoring of my good friend
Dr Phil Harker over several decades. His extraordinary wisdom has
been an inspiration.

I have been also influenced by the prolific writings of Dorothy
Rowe. She is such a sensitive and practical psychologist who, like Phil,
embellishes her insights with many anecdotal vignettes from her clinical
practice. I am particularly grateful to her for defining the depressive's
world view which I have drawn on in the text.

Another to make an impression on me was Dr Martin Seligman.
I attended one of his master classes and have read several of his books.
Seligman is a proponent of positive psychology. Frustrated by a profession
that seemed entirely dedicated to helping people with pathology suffer

less, he has been at the forefront of using psychology to help ordinary people (i.e. those without significant psychological problems) lead happier lives.

I would also like to acknowledge the influence of the French geneticist and Buddhist monk, Matthieu Ricard. His book, "Happiness" is indeed an inspiration.

I have observed the impacts of depression on loved ones and experienced the frustration of not being able to help when their worldviews seemed so greatly out of kilter. I have wished for the wisdom of Augustus in dealing with this frustration. I have come to understand that many of our psychological problems can be attributed to our inappropriate worldviews and in particular how we view ourselves and others.

When thinking about the human condition and our ability to cope, I am drawn to the words of William Glasser. Glasser said, "All psychological problems, from the slightest neurosis to the deepest psychoses are symptomatic of the frustration of this fundamental human need for a sense of personal worth. The depth and duration of the symptomatic problem (phobias, guilt, complexes, paranoia, etc) are only indicative of the depth and duration of the deprivation of self esteem."

Or as Phil Harker puts it, "Psychological adjustment occurs when people have first come to know themselves, then accept themselves and finally forget themselves."

Those suffering from depression are self-obsessed and thus find it impossible to 'forget' themselves. This is not something they consciously set out to do but comes from the natural defense mechanisms the mind puts in place when the world view it has created is not aligned with reality.

In the short story that follows you will see how the Buddhist adeptly changes the thinking of the Princess and focuses on enhancing her positive psychology.

If you are in the prison of depression, I can only hope that this little tale may help you in some way to find the key to your release. I do not say this lightly because I know how difficult that is. It is hard for many to escape the prison, because even if it is an unhappy place, it provides security and comfort in its own painful way. The only consolation is that you, quite unconsciously, constructed the prison. Some of you with courage and support will subsequently be able to tear it down, and find, as the Princess did, your own "special place".

INTRODUCTION

"One thing, all things:
move among and intermingle
without distinction.
To live in this realization
is to be without anxiety about non-perfection."

Seng-Ts'an, *Ch'an Master*

The scene was the marketplace in the city of Moluktan. The people had gathered around a short man of oriental appearance sitting cross-legged on the paving. His name was Augustus, and despite his Latin name he was a Buddhist. Augustus sat quietly in the midst of the townspeople. He was well-respected by them and he in turn loved their simplicity and their community spirit. His serenity was obvious and was manifested in the contented smile on his face.

The people had come initially to hear from a famous Mullah who was travelling through the precinct. The Mullah had spoken to the assembled crowd and had reminded them of some of the principal sayings of the Prophet. The people listened attentively hoping that their exposure to the Mullah would increase their piousness. The Mullah was a learned man who quoted extensive passages from the Koran, as well as the sayings of the Prophet. As he finished his homily, he reminded the gathering that the Prophet was reputed to have said, "Riches are not from abundance of worldly goods, but from a contented mind." The Mullah then bowed to the populace and took his leave.

Many of those in the gathering then started talking among themselves. What did he mean? Surely a 'contented mind' was a metaphor for happiness. They all desired that, but he had not given any instructions on how it might be achieved. They felt somewhat deflated by the fact that the Mullah had encouraged an aspiration without a solution.

Augustus had sat among them listening to the Mullah. The populace seemed frustrated by what had been told them. Finally one of the women asked the Buddhist, "Tell us Augustus, what is the secret of happiness."

Augustus chuckled. "There is no secret," he responded. "There are three plain steps to happiness."

"And what are they?" she enquired.

"Firstly," he said, "You must savour and caress each pleasure. When you partake of drink, sip it slowly and pause often to appreciate its flavour. When you eat your food, eat carefully and ponder over each mouthful how savoury and unique it is. Linger in the embrace of your loved ones and rejoice in their love. Cease the traffic of your mind so that you can hear the songs of birds and ingest the beauties of nature. Stop and smell the flowers one by one and put aside life's seeming imperative to hurry. When you examine a flower, notice every petal and every nuance of colour. When you are resting, remember and resavour the joys of your day. Experience each joy slowly and manifold. This is what in my tradition is called 'mindfulness'. But this in itself whilst useful and pleasant does not lead to long-term happiness. There are two further steps we must take to that end."

"Secondly," continued the little Buddhist, "You must discover the essence of your being and bestow it on the world. Strive to use, test and enhance those special talents and strengths you possess by engaging them in your discourse with the world. When you do this time flies without your awareness and your resilience builds so that when adversity comes you can be strong. When you exercise the essence of your being in this way, your sense of self will merge into the world."

"Finally, and perhaps most importantly, devote yourself to a cause that is greater than yourself. Pursue a life of meaning and purpose. Cultivate altruism and compassion. Thus life will be full and meaningful and you will lie content on your death bed."

He paused awhile in thought. The townspeople awaited his words. Then someone called out. "And which of these three processes is most important?"

Augustus responded, "Of these three steps all are important. However it is the last two which contribute most to enduring happiness. They are also the most difficult."

"Firstly, with respect to our strengths, we are so often advised not to indulge them but to bolster our weaknesses. Whilst it is helpful to be aware of our weaknesses this should not constrain us from employing our particular strengths."

"Similarly our society often models how to be self-serving rather than to pursue a higher purpose. True happiness comes when we are able to put the self aside—indeed forget the self. This is the most important step. There is no likelihood that someone who is self-obsessed could ever achieve an enduring sense of well-being."

"One of the determining features of our humanity is our consciousness. Because we are conscious we have to deal with an external world," said Augustus gesturing to the world around him, "and an internal world." He tapped his forehead as he said this.

"Instinctively, we tend to put all our hopes and fears in the outer world. Yet we are erroneous in believing this is where our sense of well-being is derived. We are faced with the dilemma that our control over the world is limited, temporary and often illusory. Although outer conditions matter to some extent and we should do what we can to improve them, ultimately it is the mind that translates those outer conditions into happiness or suffering. In fact our sense of well-being is determined by how our minds perceive and translate that outer world. And indeed our minds have the capacity to override our external conditions."

"Nevertheless, if you would but follow the path I have described, happiness is attainable. Because we are human we will sometimes forget these steps and we will have moments of suffering and sadness. But stepping back into the process allows us to be soon restored."

"Happiness, however," he warned, "Is not achieved by pursuing it for its own sake. It is the outcome of being engrossed meaningfully in life and forgetting the self."

CHAPTER 1

"No pessimist ever discovered the secrets of the stars, or
sailed to an uncharted land, or opened a new heaven to the
human spirit."

Helen Keller

The palace of the Sultan was an impressive structure, with granite walls and marble staircases, numerous bedchambers and staterooms, a throne room and a feasting hall. The high walls and imposing gates with their turbaned guards prevented unauthorised entry. The palace regally reflected the magnificence of the Sultan. Behind the palace, but still within the walled enclosure, was a spacious garden. Here there were tropical flowering trees, frangipanis and poincianas, and flowering shrubs, such as hibiscus and azaleas. In this arid landscape the gardens were an oasis for birdlife. The air was full of the sounds of a wide variety of species ranging from the melodious twitterings of honeyeaters to the harsh screeches of parrots. There were ponds full of colourful fish and a fountain. This was a truly beautiful place, emanating peace and serenity.

Sitting at the rear of the garden was an attractive young woman with her head in her hands. She had a beautiful face but the weight of depression had made it contort such that its natural beauty was disfigured with sadness. Her eyes were red and she rocked gently from side to side. It seemed so incongruous that in the midst of this beauty and plenty such sorrow could reside. This was Naomi, the princess, daughter of Salazar, the Sultan. Her world was indeed a sorrowful place and seemed to affirm her unworthiness. It had alienated her so much that she now was reluctant to engage it. As a result, she tried to remove herself as often as possible from the day to day exigencies of life. But most distressing was her underlying belief that whatever was wrong, it was really her fault.

The Sultan loved his daughter very much. He was greatly distressed by her depression. When he had first noticed her sadness he had attempted to cheer her by bringing her exotic gifts. He had sought out the most divine confectionaries and lavished her with them. When he gave them to her she smiled and partook of the delicacies but their effect was minimal and short-lived. Soon she was depressed again and her well-meaning father knew not how to distract her from her melancholy. He tried flowers and jewelry, but no matter how exquisite they were, there was never any long-term benefit.

In time, the sultan began to think of other distractions he could provide. He engaged a magician who was vastly entertaining and displayed many tricks that amused her and challenged her thinking. But some hours after his magnificent display she was as depressed as ever.

He engaged the most gifted musicians to come and perform for her. She was greatly engrossed by the music (she herself played the flute) but unfortunately soon after the performance she was again sad.

Whatever the Sultan, her father, did to try and engage her the impact soon wore off and Naomi quickly relapsed into depression. When she contemplated on her worldly circumstances she was convinced that she was inadequate to meet the challenges of her day to day existence. Her exalted position in her society only seemed to magnify her sense of unworthiness.

Whilst she had been a very serious little girl, the symptoms of depression had not become evident until she was perhaps fourteen or fifteen years old. She went for periods of time when she shunned all company and withdrew to her bedchamber, refusing to be coaxed out by her handmaidens. Even her father, the Sultan, could not persuade her to join him for a meal or to meet with friends. She remained alone weeping.

Naomi had an unhappy childhood. She was an only child and her mother had died when she was only seven years old. When her mother died people commented how stoic Naomi had been, how mature and how brave. Indeed she had provided consolation to her father, who was devoted to her. As time went by the Sultan doted on her because she was the loving legacy his wife had left him and the Princess's beauty and love was the prime remembrance and the greatest gift his wife could have bestowed on him.

She learnt to be a dutiful daughter and attend functions with her father where she was often the centre of attention because of her beauty and her precociousness. And indeed she was precocious! She could dance well and play the flute brilliantly. Her father often asked her to perform to amuse his guests. She was very intelligent and could have deep conversations with adults concerning many topics. She was an avid learner and her intellect was well-stimulated, having been provided with the best tutors and teachers.

In her early life there were few children, just adoring adults. Whilst she had many expensive toys, she had few children to play with. She did however, have one friend.

When she was about nine or ten years old, her father inducted a new official into his court. The new appointee occupied one of the senior positions. Therefore, as was his entitlement, he moved into the palace and occupied accommodation set aside for court officials. He was accompanied by his wife and his young daughter, Asma. Asma was of comparable age to Naomi. They were indeed the only children in the palace and therefore it was certain that sooner or later they would find each other. When they did, they became good friends. Whilst they were instructed that it was unbecoming to play in the palace, they met often in the palace gardens. Then just for a little while, Naomi could just be a little girl—not a princess, not someone bereaved from the loss of a mother, not a precocious musician, not someone required to entertain the court. Understandably, these were joyous times for her. And Asma was a lovely compassionate, joyful playmate. Therefore it was not surprising that Naomi came to love her.

But then as she got older, the Princess became more reluctant to engage in such conversations as had entertained her father's guests. She would sit at the table and not converse with anyone at all. She still read and she was still curious when it came to her studies, but it was as if all her contemplation was internalized and that it became too much effort, perhaps too painful, to expose herself to the exterior world. Over time even her curiosity began to diminish.

Apart from her father, the only other person that could seem to reach her was her childhood friend Asma. Because of this relationship the Sultan appointed Asma as handmaiden to the Princess.

Overriding all Naomi's concerns was the desire to please. Even though her mother had departed, she had learnt strong lessons about what her mother felt was "good" or "bad". In all her endeavours, she strived to do those things her mother had impressed on her were "good". She had understood quite clearly what was required to please her mother and her mother rewarded her for being "good". But now as she grew older there was a broader community she felt she had to please and it was not always clear how to please them. Every day became a struggle to be good enough to gain the approval of those around her. Because the task was becoming so ambiguous and the scope of those she felt compelled to please so broad, it now seemed to her impossible to cope. And worse still, her overwhelming sense of pressure and inevitable failure was not even comprehended rationally. It had been subsumed into her subconscious and manifested itself as depression. The only thing of which she was constantly conscious, was her apparent failure. And being the good child she was, she could not excuse this away. There was no doubt in her own mind that she was personally responsible for these perceived shortcomings.

CHAPTER 2

> "You, your life and the world are not fixed, unalterable
> parts of reality which you have to put up with and cope
> with as best you can. What you see as being you, your life
> and the world is not reality. You, your life and the world
> are matters that you can change."
>
> Dorothy Rowe

The Sultan became increasingly concerned about his daughter. He would try to humour, cajole and to lead her into a better frame of mind. But this was all to no avail.

It then occurred to him that perhaps there was something physically amiss with the girl. Despite her protestations, he asked the royal physician to examine her and ascertain what was wrong with his beloved daughter. In the end the physician reported back to the Sultan, "There is nothing I can determine that is physically wrong with the Princess. There is no physical causation for her sadness and her lassitude. I have exhausted all the options I know as a physician to diagnose her problem without any conclusive outcome. Perhaps you should consult the apothecary."

Accordingly the Sultan commanded the apothecary to come to the palace and examine the princess. After a cursory examination the apothecary was robust and confident in his response. "The Princess," he declared, "is suffering from a deficiency which invariably causes sadness. I am sure I can provide her with a draught which if taken regularly will restore her to happiness. But first I must consult with her further to confirm my diagnosis. The Sultan was greatly heartened by this prognosis and gave the apothecary permission to consult with his daughter.

The apothecary sat before the Princess. "Can you tell me why you are unhappy, Princess?" he enquired.

The Princess paused awhile and then responded, "You are mistaken, sir—I am not unhappy. When I was unhappy others could cheer me. It seems they can no longer do that. When I was merely unhappy the love and concerns others had for me was a great comfort. That is no longer the case. It seems I am now am imprisoned in a sorrowful place where no one can touch me. My internment makes me impervious to all their best wishes and good intentions. Even when I am in the fields and under the open blue sky, I seem to be still submerged in darkness and gloom. Whatever it is, this condition muddies my rationality and despite the most congenial of circumstances I can find nothing that would cheer me. Worst of all, when I am rational, I know that I have constructed this prison for myself."

"Then I have good news for you. My experience from many such cases leads me to believe that your condition is merely a reflection of a physical deficiency that I can rectify with a draught that I can brew from my herbs and salts."

Naomi's eyes flickered for a second. Then she frowned. "This can't be true," she responded.

The apothecary protested, "I am a respected practitioner, your highness. I have had much experience in these things. You can have faith in me."

The Princess seemed somewhat placated by this. "I trust you are right." She said, "But I can not help but believe that the essence of this problem comes from deep inside my mind. I do not think it is my body that needs medication."

"But Princess, you must understand how closely the body and the mind are interrelated. The draught I shall provide you will change the chemistry of your body which in turn will impact on your mind."

"That is plausible—but I must say I am still a little skeptical. Nevertheless there seems no harm in trying your remedy. Prepare it and I will take it."

"You will not regret it, Your Highness. Your sadness will soon be exorcised."

The apothecary went off to prepare his concoction. He found the requisite herbs and salts and weighed them out carefully on his scales. He then combined them and ground them to a paste in a mortar and pestle. Finally he added a potent liqueur and having mixed the contents well and shaken them vigorously poured them into a vial and closed it with a glass stopper. He felt confident that his formula would bring relief to the Princess.

The next morning he returned with the vial full of brown liquid. He measured out the required draught and the Princess swallowed it without demur. "There," said the apothecary, "within two days you should feel the difference."

Strangely, right away Naomi felt somewhat better. Yet there seemed to be nothing different in how her body felt—the difference was in her thinking. A feature of her depression was that she would get lost in despair, a despair that would never allow anticipation of improvement. Surely the eminent apothecary knew what he was doing and there was now hope for her. But the new found optimism was soon displaced. Inexorably the black gloom crept back and at the end of the two days where alleviation had been promised dark despair had re-established itself.

The apothecary came on the second day to appraise the success of his intervention. But when he approached the princess's chamber he could hear her muffled sobs and knew immediately that he had failed. He could not bear to face her and slunk off despondently without having to endure the pain of engaging with her in her depression.

CHAPTER 3

Your vision will become clear
Only when you look into your own heart.
Who looks outside dreams.
Who looks inside awakes.

Carl Jung, *Letters*, Volume 1

The Sultan was at his wit's end. He so dearly loved Naomi that it upset him completely to see the ongoing suffering that she endured. "What profit is there in being a Sultan," he asked himself, "if the one I hold so dear cannot be relieved of her anguish?" His courtiers could see his discomfiture and tried to console him. They admired their Sultan for his magnanimity and his genuine concern for his subjects. They were frustrated that they could not ease his pain.

Finally the Grand Vizier, who was the highest official in the Sultan's court said, "We must find someone to help our Lord. Go forth amongst the populace and seek out the sages, those of wisdom and knowledge, and try to find someone who can help the Princess escape her distress."

The Sultan's courtiers travelled throughout the land seeking to find a sage with the capacity to cure the Princess of her depression. After a time one bought a dervish back to the Sultan's court. He was a wild looking man who had been found in a cave in the mountains to the North. The villagers who lived nearby attested to his great powers. He was known to have cured the sick and was rumoured to be able to make it rain in times of drought. He had taken a vow of poverty and lived in great austerity. He appeared before the Sultan wearing only a rough robe made of animal skins and carrying a staff.

The Sultan asked, "Can you cure the princess of her depression?"

The dervish looked somewhat disdainfully at the grand Sultan. "My calling is to help the poor and the downtrodden. This is why I have taken a vow of poverty so that I might have no more than the poorest man and thus understand the rigours of poverty. You do not seem, somehow, to fall into that category."

A steely look came over the Sultan's face. "Well, you are mistaken. I ask you nothing for myself because I am, indeed, neither poor nor downtrodden. Yet my daughter, the Princess, is decidedly so. She is poor in spirit and has shown no sign of happiness for a considerable time. She is also downtrodden. And who is it that insults her? Unfortunately, the one that demeans her is the one that has greatest hold over her—namely, herself! It seems to me that the greatest contributor to her condition is the fact that she is unable to love herself. Now, I can't compel you to treat her, nor is it in my nature to do so, but I say unto you, here is someone as deserving of your intervention as anyone you might have met, whether in this cloistered place or in the meanest hamlet!"

The sage was nonplussed. "Perhaps," he said, "your daughter is deserving of my ministrations. I will try to help her."

The Sultan had the man led to a small private room near his own bedchamber. A sentry was placed on guard outside the room and the Sultan instructed that he not allow anyone else to enter and then brought the princess reluctantly into the room. "This, my dear," he said, "is a man I believe may be able to help you. Take heed of what he has to say."

The princess seemed physically repulsed by the appearance of this strange man, but she was obedient to the Sultan. "Yes, father," responded Naomi quietly.

The dervish broke into fervent chanting. Gradually his body began to move to the measure of his repetitive intonations. Very soon he was in a self-induced hypnotic trance. The Princess watched all of this dispassionately. In this trance-like state the dervish lost all sense of conventional deportment and his actions and his intonations got wilder and wilder. Despite his passionate engagement in this process, the Princess was not moved at all, but was overcome with revulsion at his aberrant behaviour. He began whirling and cavorting. As he did so, his cloak rose like a great parachute rising higher and higher as the speed of his movement increased.

To Naomi it was a frightening sight. The obsessed man's eyes rolled and his face contorted. This was all very repugnant to her but she refrained from displaying her abhorrence in deference to her father. And then at the height of his passion and fervour, the dervish called to Naomi, "Cease your suffering! Your pain has no foundation!"

She shuddered at the dervish's antics. The Princess thought how confronting and ridiculous this wild man seemed and without further thought she rushed from the room in distress and returned to her chamber.

Her father sped after her. "Naomi, Naomi," he cried. "Listen to the dervish. His techniques might be unusual but there is evidence that he can cure"

The Princesses eyes grew moist for she dearly loved her father.

"Papa, this man has no capacity to engage with me. It is possible that he has been able to help others but do not insult me by making me be subjected to his irrational rantings."

She ran into her bedchamber and flung herself onto her bed and was convulsed with loud sobbing.

The poor, distraught Sultan hung his head and walked to her side and put his arms around his beloved daughter and unashamedly wept.

The Grand Vizier had followed soundlessly behind. His heart was moved by the Sultan's distress. As he diplomatically retreated he resolved to do what he may to ease the suffering of the Sultan and his daughter.

Surely there must be some way to bring relief to the princess? He must leave no stone unturned until he found the solution to this intransigent problem. Over the coming months he quietly consulted with all the sages, the mullahs and the physicians that he personally knew. But it was all to no avail. The princess seemed irrevocably mired in her despair and to his great dismay the Sultan, himself, seemed daily to be dragged lower by the weight of his daughter's suffering.

CHAPTER 4

"If we had no winter, the spring would not be so pleasant;
if we did not sometimes taste of adversity, prosperity
would not be so welcome."

Anne Bradstreet

The Sultan little by little retreated from his court. He only appeared for the most important of occasions and all his subjects could see the growing abject sadness that he portrayed. The Sultan was well-loved, for he was wise and beneficent and his courtiers and those of his subjects that had occasion to deal with him, began to grow more and more concerned for him.

It was the Sultan's habit once a year, to entertain representatives from the farthest corners of his realm. They came to honour his contributions to the poorest and most remote subjects of his suzerainty. The representatives had come together and among them was a chieftain from one of the Sultan's westernmost provinces. The chieftain, called Yusuf, brought some simple gifts—artifacts created by the artisans of his village. The Sultan was moved by the generosity of spirit and the robust good humour of someone who seemingly had so little. The chieftain prostrated himself before the Sultan and thanked him for his generosity and concern for the people of his village.

The Sultan was a little embarrassed by the chieftain's outpourings of gratitude and his humble demeanour. "No, please arise, Yusuf. There is no need to grovel in front of me in this way. Your people have always been loyal and industrious. They have deserved every consideration I have given them. Convey to them my love and regard. I thank you for coming so far to be with me. When we sit at table this evening and break bread together to celebrate the shared benefits of our relationship, be assured there will be nobody with higher status than yourself. It is the merit of your people and their wise leaders, such as yourself, who provide the glue that has held my realm together these so many years. I must now greet others who have also come from afar. But I invite you, when we eat tonight to sit next to me and tell me of the achievements and the issues of your community."

The chieftain was profuse in his thanks and went off elated by the Sultan's invitation singing his praise of the Sultan to anyone who might listen.

In the evening the guests assembled in the most splendid of the banquet halls. The night was balmy and full of opportunities. The regional guests, excited by the Sultan's attention, arrived early and marvelled at the splendid architecture, the glorious furnishings and the sumptuous feast that was being prepared. They milled around in the banquet hall talking politely to one another. Just before the appointed time the Grand Vizier appeared. He was cognisant of the naivety of the guests and called them together.

"My friends welcome," he said. "Tonight you are blessed with the company of the Sultan, his court and his daughter, the Princess. They will soon arrive and take their place at table. Do not be overwhelmed; but there are some protocols that we would consider appropriate. Firstly you may sit at any of the tables except those who have been selected to join the Sultan and his daughter. There is a prescribed seating at the Sultan's table and I and my colleagues will help those sitting there to find their places. Show courtesy and deference to those of the Sultan's court. The Sultan has great admiration for you who have come so far and have maintained your steadfast loyalty to him. Do not be afraid to approach him and converse with him. He greatly enjoys such discourse. I would offer just a note of warning, however. Do not approach the Princess unless she encourages it. The Princess is unwell and is not normally inclined to converse with those who are not close to her."

This caused the chieftains to look quizzically at each other. The Grand Vizier continued, "I say welcome again and may you enjoy your evening."

Soon after, members of the Sultan's court began to filter into the banquet hall. They politely struck up conversation with their visitors. Not long after, the Grand Vizier appeared again, escorting the Sultan into the hall. "Behold, my friends, here is the Sultan!"

The Sultan smiled broadly at his guests and they heartily applauded him. "And now let me introduce to you the royal Princess Naomi." With this the Princess slowly entered the hall. It was apparent that she was not comfortable in the company of these strange folk that her father had assembled. She was demure and pretty, but her eyes revealed her discomfiture and her reluctance. There was no disguising the Princess's distress. Naomi's countenance reflected her melancholy for all to see. The gathering politely applauded her as well.

Then they sat down to dine. As he had promised, the Sultan had the western chieftain on his right while his daughter sat upon his left. The chieftain was overwhelmed by the honour of being next to his Sultan and initially found it difficult to make conversation. But the Sultan was most empathetic, and sensing the reluctance of the chieftain, was proactive in engaging him. In a short while they had exchanged all the details of their families and their personal biographies and were quickly comfortable with each other.

Out of politeness, the chieftain tried to converse with the princess. "I have heard, Your Highness, that you are an accomplished musician. Will you be playing for us tonight?"

The princess looked briefly at him and then averted her gaze. "No sir, I can not."

The princess looked so sad and distracted that the chieftain was loath to speak to her in response.

He returned his attention to the Sultan. Soon after, having eaten only a morsel or two, the princess begged her leave to withdraw.

When she had left the table, the chieftain enquired of the Sultan, "Is the princess unwell?"

The Sultan sighed. "Well, yes she is, my friend, but perhaps in a way you may not understand."

"How so my lord?"

"Well the princess suffers from depression. It is not an ailment you can easily put a finger to. She spends her days overcome by melancholy. It is such a burden to see her so immersed in her sadness."

The chieftain could see the depth of his Sultan's compassion and the sorrow that the affliction had caused him.

"I only wish I knew how to rid her of this affliction. I have brought physicians, apothecaries and sages to her—but none have been able to relieve her melancholy." He sighed, and his concern was apparent.

"If only I could find someone to help her." He turned and looked at the chieftain. "You know," he said, "I am a Sultan and command great resources. My frustration arises from the fact that despite my status and the wealth of my kingdom, the thing that means most to me—the welfare of my daughter—is seemingly beyond my reach. Would that I could find someone or some technique to rid her of her sorrow. I would give my suzerainty to free her from her sadness."

The chieftain hung his head in empathy with the Sultan's sorrow. After awhile he looked into the Sultan's eyes and said, "Maybe, your majesty, there is someone who can relieve your daughter's pain."

"I know you mean well," said the Sultan, "But don't fill me with false hope. The others who were brought to my court to aid the Princess, came also with the recommendations of such as you. But none of them have improved her condition one iota. Don't disappoint me again."

The chieftain hesitated and then went on. "Lord, I would not wish it upon you to give you false hope. But there is a man in my community that has the capacity to make people whole and to improve their well-being. He does not seek recognition for his efforts—in fact he recoils from acclaim—but he has done much to mend those who suffer and has sought to make the lives of ordinary people happier. I warn you that he is not of our faith, but his compassion and concern are legendary. He is the only one I know who might ease the suffering of your daughter. His name is Augustus."

The Sultan sighed. "I thank you sir, for this information. If I knew another way, indeed I would use it. If there is the slightest chance that your Augustus can help I must take it. That is indeed a strange name. I have never heard of anyone called that before."

Yusuf nodded. "He believes his father was a student of history and named him after a famous emperor from the Western tradition. But as you say, it is not a name common in our society."

The Sultan beckoned the Grand Vizier to come to him. "The chieftain here believes there is a man in his village that can help the Princess, Naomi. Will you have him brought to me?"

The Grand Vizier raised his eyebrows in surprise but then quickly responded. "Of course, Lord. I will set out, myself, tomorrow."

CHAPTER 5

"To give up yourself without regret is the greatest charity."
Bodhidharma

The following morning, the Grand Vizier set off with the chieftain and two attendants to travel to the chieftain's village, Moluktan. For three days they rode at a steady pace. The country became more dry and barren as they progressed. If it had not been for the local knowledge of the chieftain, they would not have been able to find feed and water for their horses when they tethered them at night

But on the fourth day they traversed a rocky spur following a difficult but well-used track that in places was so confined by the rocky ramparts that it was something of a squeeze to allow the occasional traveller coming from the other direction to pass. Late morning they crested the spur and the chieftain drew the party to a halt. Turning to the Grand Vizier, the chieftain pointed into the distance and said, "There, sir, is our destination. That is Moluktan."

They looked down below, where the path broke out from the rocky escarpment onto a broad, well-grassed plain. In the middle distance was a tree-lined river which came from the north but then turned and flowed west. Perhaps, ten or twelve kilometres from where they stood they could plainly see a small town with mud-brick dwellings, some of which were whitewashed and quite conspicuous in the bright sunlight. Towering above the motley array of mud brick houses was a minaret atop a domed mosque.

The precipitous downward part of the track was difficult to traverse. Consequently, some hours passed before they drew near to the town. As they approached Moluktan they could hear the Muezzin calling the faithful to prayer, "Allahu Akbar!"

The travellers joined the villagers in the mosque for their afternoon prayers. Afterwards, the chieftain said to the Grand Vizier, "Now we must find the little Buddhist."

He led them through the tortuous maze of streets and alleyways that allowed the citizens to do commerce in the city's centre. They progressed until the greater part of the city was behind them. Finally, on the western extremity, they came to a tiny cottage. There was a pretty little flower garden at the front, some fruit trees at the side and a vegetable plot at the rear. Beyond the vegetable plot was an enclosure with a few goats and another with eight or nine chickens. The goat and chicken enclosures were shaded under the left hand side of a large poinciana tree. Under the right side of the tree, on a patch of grass in the shade, sat a sturdy little figure in a saffron robe, cross-legged on the ground. Pointing at the figure, the chieftain said, "There is Augustus."

The Grand Vizier gazed at the motionless Buddhist. He turned to the chieftain. "What is he doing?"

"He calls it his 'practice'. Others, I have heard, call it meditation. Shall I fetch him for you?"

"No, don't disturb him. We will wait until he is finished." They tethered their horses and found a patch of shade. There they sat and chatted quietly. Presently, Augustus stood and looking around saw the waiting group and the familiar face of the chieftain.

Augustus's face broke into a smile. "Ah, Yusuf—you have brought me company!"

"Yes, Augustus, this is Abdullah, the venerable Grand Vizier who has come all the way from the Sultan's palace to speak with you."

Surprise fleetingly showed on the young man's face. "It astonishes me Yusuf that anyone from the Sultan's palace would even know of my existence."

The Grand Vizier interceded. "I have come to seek assistance from you Augustus, because Yusuf has told us of your ability to heal others."

Augustus frowned.

"Then Yusuf has misled you, for I am no healer."

The Grand Vizier was nonplussed by this response.

Yusuf hastened to justify himself. "Oh come Augustus, many have benefited from your ministrations."

"Then you have misunderstood my work, Yusuf. As a Buddhist monk I have vowed to do what I can to ease the suffering of the world. But it would be a gross exaggeration to call me a healer."

"How do you help them ease their suffering?" asked the Grand Vizier.

"I help them by leading them to more appropriate ways of viewing the world and interpreting their lives. You see, most of what happens to us in life we have no choice over. What we do have choice over is how we interpret what happens. Many of us suffer needless distress because we have learnt, through no fault of our own, to see the world, and our part in it, in dysfunctional ways. I can not heal these people for there is no wound to heal. I can only help them see things in a more appropriate way and that, by itself, assists them to change their behaviour for the better. I can only facilitate a process which of necessity sees them solve their own problem. And I hasten to add I offer no magic cures or 'quick fixes'."

The Grand Vizier, who was himself a wise and compassionate man, was intrigued by the words of the Buddhist.

"Well, little master, whether you call yourself healer or not, you are pledged to alleviate suffering. I have someone very special who is suffering. And I beseech you to help us alleviate her suffering."

"Who is this 'special' someone, that you should come so far to seek my aid?"

"The one I would have you minister to, is Naomi, the Princess, daughter of the Sultan."

"She is no more 'special' to me than the peasant girl who lives in the house across the street," responded Augustus, pointing at a hut nearby.

Yusuf seemed incensed by Augustus's remark but the Grand Vizier silenced him and continued.

"But you do not understand, Augustus. Because of the distress of the Princess the Sultan is distracted. The Sultan is benevolent and caring of his subjects but he can not minister to them properly in the state that he is in. I am not merely asking you to care for the Princess. I fear if her malady is not cured the whole Suzerainty will suffer. Surely that is significant enough for you to want to render assistance."

Augustus stayed silent for a while. Then he looked the Grand Vizier in the eye and said, "You have put a good case sir and my intuition tells me you are one that can be trusted. I will try to help."

"Thank you Augustus. You will have not only my gratitude and the Sultan's gratitude but the thanks of the whole country."

"Gratitude is a noble quality sir, and it springs from good will and humility but it is not something I seek. Let us talk no more of gratitude but of how we might have this young lady come to a more objective view of her world. If I am to work with the Princess it will not be to receive your gratitude but to relieve her anguish. Tell me more of the Princess and her affliction."

"The physician tells us she suffers from severe depression."

"No, no, sir! It is not helpful to me to name her affliction—that will only distract and confuse us. Explain to me how she behaves."

The Grand Vizier seemed surprised at this but he thought a moment and tried to explain her behaviour.

"Over the years that I have known her, she has become more withdrawn and uncommunicative. She withdraws to her bedchamber where I often hear her sobbing. When she is in such a state, there seems there is nothing we can do to cheer her. She was always a serious young girl and didn't smile much, but when she was younger she seemed so much more engaged in life and much more optimistic. She is a pretty young woman, but when she is in the grips of the affliction, the muscles in her face seem to relax and her face sags into an ugly caricature of herself. She then sleeps much and is difficult to engage in the most basic discussion. She acts as though she believes herself unworthy and incompetent. The least difficulty then becomes insurmountable and she dissolves in self-pity and lassitude."

The Grand Vizier paused, and Augustus could see how much it pained him to describe the princess's condition. He looked imploringly at the little Buddhist.

"Perhaps the die was cast when her mother died. She was quite young and heaven knows how difficult that must be for a child. Please try to help her."

"I will," replied Augustus, "and I thank you for your vivid description of her behaviour. That has been most helpful."

"Will you return with us tomorrow to the palace so that you might start on your healing processes?"

"No, I can not," replied Augustus. "You see sir, this is an undertaking of some magnitude. I warn you it will take at least six months for my processes to have effect and it may take considerably longer than that to establish new behavioural patterns in the young lady. Consequently I must make my own arrangements to be absent for a long period of time if I am to make a lasting impact."

The Grand Vizier was a little dismayed at this prognostication. Augustus continued, "I would not even contemplate coming unless you give me at least six months to work with her. Is that acceptable to you?"

"I appreciate your honesty Augustus. And in the end, I suppose we have no choice. I will undertake that, if you come to the palace, we will provide for you for six months after which time we will review your progress and determine anything further you may need to do. Can we agree on that course of action?"

"That is fair enough," the Buddhist responded. "I will make my arrangements and join you in the palace in ten days."

CHAPTER 6

"Keep in mind that a path is only a path; if you feel you
should not follow it, you must not stay with it under any
condition. This is not an affront, to oneself or to others,
in dropping it if that is what your heart tells you to do.
But your decision to keep on the path or to leave it must
be free of fear or ambition. Try as many times as you
think necessary. Then ask yourself alone one question.
Does this path have heart? . . . . One [path] makes for a
joyful journey; as long as you follow it, you are one with
it. The other will make you curse life. One makes you
strong; the other weak."

Carlos Castaneda

The next day Augustus negotiated with his neighbours how they might
sustain his household. He left a little money so that they could purchase
feed for his goats and chickens. In return they would milk the goats and
collect the eggs for their own use. The vegetables would be tended and
harvested as they matured and the flower garden would be watered until
the flowers were spent. Augustus was greatly loved and his neighbours
were keen to ensure that they maintained his animals and gardens
and would not have asked for reward. In the end after seemingly long
negotiations, Augustus was happy that everything would be attended to
and that the neighbours would benefit from the produce of his animals
and garden. There seemed not much moment in how a few eggs, a litre
or two of milk and sundry vegetables might be disposed of. But these

were poor people and Augustus knew that a little extra to put on the table was important to them. Having settled these arrangements to his satisfaction he was now able to think of his new challenge—the princess Naomi.

The Grand Vizier, having travelled to Moluktan on horseback would not have known that Augustus intended to make his way to the palace by foot. But Augustus was resilient and determined, so that two days after the visit from the palace courtiers, he set off to fulfil his promise to be there ten days after the meeting.

Augustus loved to travel and he liked to walk. When travelling he learnt so much and when walking he had the time and the opportunity to take in his surroundings. As he progressed towards the palace, he contemplated human happiness and how it could be attained. He was adamant that when he arrived at the palace he should be prepared to engage with the Princess in a helpful way and deal with the distortions of her mind. He could only do that if his own mind was clear and prepared. His meditation practice was the mechanism to achieve these ends. In the evenings and again in the mornings he meditated on loving-kindness and compassion.

Augustus also took pleasure in walking meditation. Although it was important that he should arrive at the prescribed destination, it seemed even more important to him that he should enjoy the way. He meditated as he walked. He breathed in, in, in for three steps and out, out, out for three steps. When he silenced his internal chatter he engaged so much more with the countryside he traversed. He heard the birds sing, he noticed the trees with their diverse foliage and he delighted in every flower along the way. Wisely, he knew that this was the best preparation for the task at hand. He was cultivating his "mindfulness'.

He carried a little rucksack on his back with a few changes of clothing, some basic bedding, utensils and supplies. He loved nothing more than to spend the night by the side of a stream or under the branches of sheltering trees. He was a seasoned traveller and looked for opportunities to replenish his water supply, augment his cache of food or to find appropriate shelter. He was comfortable in the outdoors and hardly missed his little cottage, his cot and his stove. He was always optimistic that the world would provide for him and that there were lessons to be learnt from his immersion in Nature.

His progress was slow but measured. Up the escarpment he trudged. Walking meditation made him aware of the rocks, aware of the heat, aware of his exertion, but it also made him aware of his contentment. It was never any different. He was always contented when he was in the countryside, walking. Down the escarpment he trudged. Walking meditation made him aware of the shrubs at the side of the track, the vast brown plain he could sometimes see at the end of the path, but more than anything of the clear blue sky with a solitary hawk circling overhead and the joy he felt under its broad canopy.

Some days passed by. He met sundry folk along the way. Their company was a contrast to his isolation as he walked alone to the palace. Yet, nevertheless, he did not crave for it. He was just as content in his own company as he was with the companionship of the various mendicants who, perchance, crossed his path. For Augustus there were few joys that could surpass that of a stilled mind.

He had passed over the rocky highlands and was now making his way across the sunburnt barren plain that stretched for three days march before him. Because of the heat, Augustus would set off an hour or so before dawn and halt late morning to find some shade where he would rest until late afternoon. He would then walk again until an hour or two after sunset, before making camp. In this way he could conserve his energy and his water.

And thus it was, true to his word, ten days after his encounter with the Grand Vizier, Augustus strode purposefully into the city where the Sultan's palace was situated, which was called Yolanpur, and asked directions to the Sultan's Palace. He wended his way through the winding streets and congested alleyways. He stopped for a while to watch the commerce of the bazaar. There were merchants and traders, goldsmiths and spice sellers. There were also entertainers—a magician, a minstrel and a man, whose clothing and features suggested he was from a foreign country, reciting from verses from a holy tract called the Bhagavad-Gita.

He listened to the recitation, enjoying the beauty of the words and musing at the wisdom therein. He bought a few figs from a stall and sat and watched the magician amaze the crowd with his illusions. It seemed to him a worthwhile lesson to show the gullible how the illusions of the world could so easily dupe us (although the illusions he had in mind were deeper and more pervasive than those of the magician!). He smiled at the awe-struck visages of the children. Their wonder soon turned to merriment when the magician pulled an egg from one's ear and made another's hat disappear and then reappear again. The bazaar was boisterous and full of good humour.

Augustus wandered around the myriad stalls and shopfronts. Finally he saw a place that was full of mementos and ornaments. They were mostly reflecting the spiritual traditions of the East. He perused the offerings and carefully read the various samples of wisdom. There was a scroll wrapped up in a wooden cylinder. He withdrew it from its container.

> "Although you may attempt to do a hundred things in this world, only Love will give you release from the bondage of yourself."
>
> Jami
> (poet of Persia, saint and mystic)

This immediately resonated with the Buddhist and on a moment of impulse he reached into his purse, pulled out a few coins and bought it.

His Master, the sage Takygulpa Rinpoche had taught him the benefit of loving-kindness. Compassion for another not only provides comfort for the other but rebounds to the perpetrator as peace and serenity. Therefore the words of the Sufi sage had resonated with the little Buddhist.

Soon after he left the bazaar and walked to the palace.

CHAPTER 7

"The essence of the Way is detachment. And the goal of
those who practice is freedom from appearances."

Bodhidharma

Augustus walked slowly towards the palace gates. He was somewhat overwhelmed by the imposing edifice that was the Sultan's palace. He stood motionless for some time just letting his eyes scan the stone walls, the turrets and the balconies. Finally he took a deep breath and marched forward.

"Halt!" A call resounded from his left.

Stepping out from a guard post, hidden behind the wall just inside the gates, emerged a turbanned figure brandishing a scimitar.

"Who are you and what is your business here?"

Augustus was somewhat taken aback. "My name is Augustus and I was invited to come to the palace by the Grand Vizier."

The guard's brow creased with a frown. "We will need to check on that. Follow me."

He replaced his weapon into its scabbard and strode off towards the palace. They approached over a flagstoned carriageway. Then they climbed a series of steps and entered through the doors into a broad reception area. Again there were guards. The guard from the gate motioned to one of them and said, "Keep an eye on this fellow." He then approached a palace official further inside and muttered something to him that Augustus could not hear. He returned to Augustus and said, "Wait here while the Grand Vizier is summoned."

Augustus took his rucksack off and placed it on the floor and then seated himself on a bench alongside, under the watchful eye of the guard. There was a deal of activity with people coming and going. The sumptuousness of the furnishings and the number of palace attendants attested to the Sultan's great wealth. The little Buddhist sat patiently for maybe half an hour and then he saw the berobed figure of the Grand Vizier striding purposefully towards him. "Welcome, Augustus," he called across the entrance hall. His smile made it obvious that he was indeed pleased to see Augustus.

Arising from his seat, Augustus bowed in deference to the Sultan's emissary. "It is good to see you again, Abdullah."

The guards nearby, looked at each other in surprise. It was not protocol to address the Grand Vizier by name. He was normally addressed as "Your Excellency," or "Effendi". Yet he did not seem to take offence. Perhaps the little visitor had a special relationship with this high official of the Sultan's court. (But in reality Augustus knew nothing of the protocols of court, and to his credit the Grand Vizier was at ease with himself and did not seek deference and formality.)

"I trust you have had a pleasant journey?"

"Yes, I have."

"Where have you left your horse? I will send an attendant to fetch it and bring it to the palace stables."

The Buddhist smiled. "I have no horse."

The Grand Vizier was perplexed. "Then how did you travel here?"

"The way I always travel—I walked."

"That is a long walk! It took us four days with horses! You should have told me. I could have sent someone to fetch you."

"No, sir—I am glad you did not. I would not have it any other way. I like to walk. It gives me an opportunity to increase my awareness and appreciation of the countryside, to meditate and to exercise. Walking is a joy for me."

The Grand Vizier shook his head in amazement. "You must be worn out. Here let me help you to your accommodation so that you can rest a while."

Despite Augustus's protests, Abdullah picked up the little Buddhist's rucksack and led him off through the palace.

As they walked through the palace, Abdullah explained to him the various functions of the rooms and halls of the building.

"This," he said, "is where the Sultan entertains the ambassadors of other states. Here is where he presides over the feasts where he hosts the chieftains from within his suzerainty. These are the chambers where his servants live."

They walked along a hallway and finally came to a cluster of rooms that were well-appointed and lushly furnished.

"This is where the guests of the Sultan stay."

He opened a door on his left, "And this is your room."

Augustus was overwhelmed. In the room there was a bed with a splendid cover, a side table with a pitcher of water and a chest where he might stow his personal effects. Beside the chest was a free-standing full-length mirror. On one side of the bedroom was a doorway that led out to a balcony that overlooked the palace gardens. On the other side of the room, there was a lush divan covered in soft embroidered cushions. In front of it was a sturdy wooden table with two chairs. Alongside the door was a huge earthenware urn filled with cut flowers.

This was far more resplendent than Augustus's little bedroom at home with its cot and closet and a plain mat on the floor.

"Make yourself comfortable," said Abdullah. "Tomorrow I will come and get you and introduce you to the Sultan. If you need anything, there are servants outside who will attend to your needs. You must be tired after such a long walk. Rest and restore yourself. In the morn we will begin your task to rehabilitate the Princess."

Although he was inclined to protest that he was not tired, Augustus merely shrugged his shoulders and said, "I look forward to meeting the Princess on the morrow."

After he had unpacked his few belongings, Augustus sat cross-legged on the floor and meditated. After a considerable time, there came a knocking at the door. He arose and found that a servant girl stood there. "Master," she said, "the Grand Vizier requests your pleasure at dinner. Follow me."

Off went the girl with the Buddhist close behind. She led him to a private dining room where the Grand Vizier sat surrounded by a half-dozen other palace officials. Abdullah stood up and welcomed Augustus. "Come," he said, "Join us at our table. I would have you meet some of the other court officials."

They greeted Augustus with some deference. "We are grateful," said one that you have come so far to try and heal our Princess. "Her sad state is not only a source of great sorrow to us, but it is great distraction to the Sultan. He can not rule well while she is so afflicted." Some of the others nodded their heads in agreement.

"I will do what I can," said Augustus, "but I must warn you there is no sure cure. In essence I can not cure her—I can only facilitate a process whereby she may come to view the world more objectively."

"You must do what you can," said Abdullah, "but rest assured you can count on our support."

There was no more talk of the Princess. They told Augustus of the benevolence of the Sultan and described the ways of the court. As the evening progressed they became quite convivial and Augustus enjoyed their company. Finally, Augustus made a move to retire. As he took his leave, Abdullah said, "Tomorrow, I shall come to you and take you to meet the Sultan. With his agreement, you shall then meet the Princess and, with her blessing, you can begin your work."

"So be it," responded the Buddhist. "Thank you for your hospitality."

CHAPTER 8

"Learning is finding out what we already know. Doing is
demonstrating that you know it. Teaching is reminding
others that they know just as well as you. You are all
learners, doers and teachers."

Richard Bach

When Augustus awoke he found that a pitcher of water, a washbasin,
towel and soap had been placed by his door. He carried out his morning
ablutions and then assumed his meditation position cross-legged on
a mat the floor. With mind quieted, he became aware of his various
bodily sensations and the muffled sounds of activity out in the palace.
He had left the door to his balcony open and the sounds of birds in the
garden fell gently on his ears. The breeze wafted in the scent of flowers.
He was devoid of thought but full of awareness. He sat in an ocean of
blissful contentment.

Some time later there came a knock at the door. Augustus arose
and called, "Enter."

In came the servant girl he had seen the evening before. She carried
a small platter with some fruit, two pieces of unleavened bread, a little
cheese and a tumbler of water. She placed the platter on the table.

"Thank you," said Augustus, "That will surely satisfy my
hunger."

The girl smiled at the benign little man and pointing at the items
he had used to wash with asked, "Are you finished with these, sir?"
Augustus nodded his head, "Then I will clear them away for you."

"You are very kind," said Augustus.

Augustus sat for a while and slowly consumed some of the food. As was his custom he would take small bites, savour the flavour for a time, before swallowing. His meal was slow but thoroughly enjoyable. When satisfied he walked out onto his balcony and surveyed the scene. He contemplated the work he was about to begin with the Princess. He knew that he would be most effective in the role he was to play by maintaining his own serenity and equanimity.

The Palace gardens were magnificent with flowering tropical trees and shrubs, elegant palms, interspersed with paved areas, a large pond fed by a graceful fountain whose output cascaded down a series of rocks into its furtherest end. There was great contrast between the splendid ornamentation of the garden and the dusty streets outside the palace walls. There was perhaps an even greater contrast between the luxury of the palace and the modest mud brick buildings in the surrounding township.

It defied conventional wisdom with its emphasis on material acquisition to believe that someone, such as Naomi, could live amongst all this splendour and still be unhappy! On the other hand, Augustus, who was serene and contented, lived in his simple hut with but a handful of material possessions.

He knew that his greatest asset was a trained mind—a mind that had been guided and disciplined by his teachers and strengthened and expanded by his practice. His equanimity was bolstered by his detachment. Life brought to him many pleasures and he was grateful for them. But he knew that these enjoyable moments were fleeting and would soon pass. As a consequence he had learnt not to desire these ephemeral pleasures or to seek them out in the false belief that his happiness depended on them. He was pleased with the opportunity to experience pleasure but he was not foolish enough to believe his sense of well-being was dependent on such serendipitous events. His sense of personal well-being was built on a firmer foundation.

Very soon the Grand Vizier appeared and said, "The Sultan will confer with you now."

Augustus followed Abdullah through the maze of halls and passageways until they came to the throne room. There the Sultan sat, with his court surrounding him.

Abdullah approached the Sultan and then kneeled respectfully before him. "This, Sire, is Augustus, who has come to help your daughter."

The Sultan looked keenly at the little Buddhist. He then turned to his courtiers and said, "Go! I want to be alone with this man."

The courtiers seemed initially somewhat disconcerted and looked at each other in surprise; but then, in deference to the Sultan's wishes, obediently left the. Moments later there remained only the Sultan, the Grand Vizier and Augustus.

The Sultan looked tired and disillusioned. He put on a weary smile and addressed his young visitor. "Welcome to my palace, Augustus. Abdullah tells me you have come a long way to tend to my daughter. I thank you for that."

"There is no need to thank me sire, because I have not yet delivered you anything. I also caution you against holding too high hopes about what I can do for your daughter. What I am about to attempt is difficult and, even with the best will, may easily fail. As well, there is no need to thank me because it is my sworn duty to help alleviate the suffering of this world. My ambition is to relieve suffering and the cause of suffering wherever I can. It seems as though the condition of your daughter is distressing, not only to you and her, but to many of your subjects as well."

"That is true, Augustus. I am at my wit's end. I love my daughter dearly and it is heart-wrenching to see her in such a state. I am disappointed that you can not guarantee success in your attempts to relieve the suffering of Naomi. Yet, I am grateful that you are honest with me. Others that have come to ease her burden have not been so forthright. But tell me why your treatment will take so long."

Augustus paused awhile before responding. "Your daughter is ensconced in a prison of her own making. She, herself constructed it brick on top of brick. Only she can tear it down. When she does it will again be brick by brick. There is no other way."

The Sultan sighed. "I am not sure I understand you. What is this prison that constrains her."

"Well, sire, it is what you might call her worldview—the way she sees the world. When we see the world in dysfunctional ways we are destined to suffer."

"How can there be such 'worldviews'—surely there is just the world and we all see it in a similar fashion?"

"Not so, my Lord. How we perceive the world is largely determined by a whole lot of underlying assumptions and beliefs we hold. These beliefs are buried in our subconscious and we seldom question them."

Augustus thought back to a time his master Takygulpa Rinpoche had sought to teach him about worldviews.

Takygulpa Rinpoche and Augustus walked slowly along the path by the river's bank. The river was deep and the current swift. The sound of water running over the rapids further downstream carried through the evening air. "I enjoy the river," said Augustus. "I find it peaceful and enervating."

"There are many who are afraid of the river," said his master. "How do you think it is that some can look at the river and feel fear and others look at it and feel joy?"

Augustus walked on deep in thought, but without answering. "Surely the river is the river and would appear to all in the same way?" he finally ventured.

"Suppose," said his master, that you had been walking all day and finally, tired and thirsty, you arrive at the river's bank. How does it appear to you then?"

"It would be very inviting."

"On the other hand, say it was cold and wet and walking in the woods you come across a bear? The bear is angry and gives chase. You run as fast as you can but the bear is close behind. Then, you come to the river's bank where the water is wildest and the torrent swiftest. How does the river appear then?"

"It is a frightening obstruction."

"What has changed?"

"My state of mind."

"Yes. So you see, we can see things differently because of our different states of mind. Fear, in particular, distorts our viewpoint."

"It is good then that we don't often get chased by bears."

"Oh, but we do. Many of us are always being chased by bears— imaginary bears—in our minds. Or, just as fearful, anticipating being chased by bears when there are no bears. We are forever dealing with our interpretation of the world, not the world as it is. This is a major cause of suffering."

After Augustus had related this story, the Sultan smiled. "Perhaps I see what you mean. What would the so-called worldview of someone in my daughter's condition be like?"

"Well I can't say for certain, sire, but here are some things people in such a state commonly believe:

- No matter how good and acceptable I appear to be, I am really bad, evil, valueless, unacceptable to myself and other people
- Other people are such that I must fear, hate and envy them
- Life is terrible and death is worse
- Only bad things have happened to me in the past and only bad things will happen to me in the future
- I must never forgive anyone, least of all myself."

The Sultan frowned. "It is likely my daughter shares some of these beliefs."

Augustus nodded. "And you can see sire, what a depressing place a world built on such ideas might be."

"Indeed. But tell me again why might a cure, if she is to be cured, take so long."

"These beliefs have been absorbed and reinforced in her mind for many years. They are now habitual. The only way to remove such habits is to replace them with more useful ones. And this takes time."

"And you have the skill for such an undertaking?"

"If I can gain the Princess's cooperation, I believe I have."

The Sultan paused and looked towards the Grand Vizier. "Abdullah, old friend, I am not objective enough to oversee this enterprise. Can I ask you to work with Augustus to alleviate my daughter's suffering?"

"Of course my Lord. I will do all that I can."

"Augustus, what will you require of my daughter?"

"Well, Your Highness, I would like to see her twice a day—perhaps an hour in the morning and then again an hour in the evening before she retires. All I need is a quiet place where we might meet and talk."

"That is easily done. Abdullah, make a room available to Augustus in the accommodation that I reserve for visiting members of state. And

---

1   Adapted from the work of Dorothy Rowe

Augustus, you must understand the protocols of my court. The Princess can not be alone with you. She must have an attendant with her at all times."

"That is not a problem," responded Augustus. "It would be useful, however, if that person was sympathetic and discreet."

The Grand Vizier interceded. "Naomi has a close relationship with her handmaiden, Asma and the young lady has great concern for the Princess. We will ensure that she is the one to accompany the Princess."

The Sultan nodded. "So be it. When can you start, Augustus?"

"With your permission, sire, I will begin tomorrow morning."

"Good! I am pleased! We can at least try your methods. It has been so frustrating seeing her suffer and not being able to do anything about it. Abdullah, I want you to see that Augustus gets anything he needs and bring him back again to me in a month so that he might report on progress."

CHAPTER 9

"Teachers open the door. You enter by yourself."

Chinese Proverb

The next morning Augustus went to the room that the Grand Vizier had shown him the previous evening and awaited for the Princess to arrive. He sat cross-legged on the floor and meditated.

Some time later the Princess arrived, accompanied by her handmaiden, Asma. Asma said, "I will wait for you here, Your Highness." She sat down on a stool beside the door and took some material from the basket she was carrying. "I will just do some needlework." The Princess murmured her agreement.

Augustus arose from the floor and moved to greet the Princess. "Good morning," he said. "You must be the Princess Naomi." The Princess nodded. "I am Augustus and your father has asked me to work with you."

"Will you help me rid myself of this depression?" The Princess looked imploringly into the little Buddhist's face. She was a slightly built woman. She had a pretty face but much of its attractiveness was masked by her despair. Her face sagged and the cloud of her unhappiness was obvious.

"Well," he responded. "I have come to help you see the world differently."

The Princess seemed a little taken aback by this response. But before she could respond, Augustus asked, "How is your father this morning?"

Naomi looked perplexed. "I do not know. I haven't seen him yet."

"Perhaps you might seek him out and ask about his welfare."

She shrugged her shoulders. "If you think this would be helpful."

Augustus nodded and the Princess turned and left the room. Naomi's handmaiden glanced up at Augustus with an inquiring look, but then returned to her sewing. The Princess was gone but a short while. On her return she volunteered, "My father said he is well."

Augustus smiled and responded, "I am pleased. Would you come and sit near me? It is my practice to sit on the floor when I teach. If you are comfortable, I would invite you to do so as well. If you are uncomfortable sitting in this way you might prefer to sit in the chair."

"No, I am quite able to sit on a cushion on the floor. Do you want me to assume a posture like yours?"

"If that is not too difficult for you."

The Princess assumed the half-lotus position.

"What is it that you will seek to teach me? Can you teach me how to find happiness?"

"Happiness," said Augustus, "is like a cat. You can coax and cajole it but it will pay you no attention. But if you disregard it, it will soon be rubbing itself against your legs. You can not approach happiness directly. It is a consequence of largely forgetting yourself. We will begin by teaching you a process to still your mind. Our minds are largely distracted by self-talk, those voices inside our heads that are continuously urging us to denigrate ourselves and defend our self-concept. Stopping this self-talk, even for a short time, is helpful in forgetting ourselves. Those in your condition are often obsessed with their shortcomings and how others will perceive them because of these shortcomings. This often dominates their internal discourse."

Naomi hung her head, obviously ruminating on these words. "You are right. This is the continuing cause of my distress. How will you teach me to be otherwise?"

"I am not a conventional teacher. I do not have facts to convey to you. There are no texts, no syllabus. I am just seeking to have you come to a more constructive world view. So, to enable us to do that, we will first take a little time to learn a way of stilling your mind and increasing your awareness. But I can't do anything without your cooperation. Therefore if you don't agree we will look to do something else."

She looked intently at the smiling little man. She could sense his compassion. She felt comfortable and in control in his presence. The memories of the apothecary and the dervish came flooding back. He was not trying to manipulate her to do things against her will.

"No, I am happy to work with you and follow your suggestions. I am ready to try something different. There must be a way for me to overcome this demon, to escape from this bleak prison. I am ready."

The Buddhist nodded his head. "In my tradition it is said that when the pupil is ready, the teacher shall appear. The prison you speak of is of your own making. It is designed not to keep you in, but to keep the world out. You have not constructed it consciously, but once you are aware that it is of your own construction then you can soon believe that you have the wherewithal to deconstruct it. This behaviour of yours is a coping mechanism. It constructs a place that you withdraw to when reaching out to others has become too painful. But do not let this concern you. First let us learn how to meditate."

In the next half-hour or so, Augustus instructed the Princess in a basic meditation technique. He taught her how to concentrate on her breathing, to notice the in-breath and the out-breath, to put aside thoughts as they arose and to empty her mind. They finished by meditating together.

"That is enough," Augustus said quietly rising from the floor.

He extended a hand to help the Princess stand as well.

"What now?" she asked.

He laughed. "Nothing now. If you feel so inclined, practice your meditation when you may, and come again and see me this evening."

"That is the first time for some years that my mind was not full of negative thoughts. It was a great relief."

"That is only the beginning," said Augustus, "and while that has given you temporary relief, it is not the cure. One day, when you are ready, I will show you the way to a special place—a place where you will find peace."

The Princess was intrigued. "Where is this place? Is it far away?"

"Oh no," smiled Augustus. "It is closer than you know. One of the sages from my tradition said 'Not knowing how near the truth is, people seek it far away,—what a pity! They are like one who, in the midst of water, cries imploringly for a drink of water.' This special place is like that."

The Princess shrugged her shoulders. "You talk in riddles, Augustus."

"Perhaps, Princess."

"Is there not a more rational explanation of your methods?"

Augustus sighed. "Our rationality can only take us so far. It is though on our journey we have to first cross a lake. Our rationality could be viewed as the boat which enables us to cross the lake. But when we get to the other side there is further to travel. To get to our destination we must leave the boat behind and traverse the forest and climb the mountain."

Naomi just shook her head. "I do not understand. You have confused me."

"No matter," responded Augustus. "You do not have to understand. This is not an intellectual exercise. The success of our journey will depend more on what you experience rather than what you understand."

CHAPTER 10

"Virtue extends our days: he lives two lives who relives his
past with pleasure."

Marcus Valerius Martialis

The evening was cool and Augustus was, as always, at ease. He was optimistic that as a result of his first session with the Princess he had made some progress. Again he sat on the floor and meditated as he waited her arrival.

Shortly after, Naomi and her handmaiden arrived. As in the morning the hand maiden took a seat by the door and resumed her needlework The Princess strode towards Augustus and after a perfunctory greeting took up her position on the floor opposite him.

"Good evening, Princess. I am pleased that you could come again."

"What is it that you would have us do this evening?" enquired the Princess.

"Let us meditate again awhile," said Augustus. Again they went through the practice of noticing the breath—the in-breath and the out-breath—and silencing the self-talk that tried to impose on the natural equanimity of the meditative state.

After twenty minutes or so, Augustus roused himself. He turned to the Princess and said, "Bring your mind to attention. Ready your body. Stretch and come gently again into the sensate world."

Naomi followed his instructions and gradually brought herself back into conscious awareness of where she was and what she was doing.

After a time she looked at the little Buddhist who still sat motionless in his lotus position. "What now?" she asked.

"Now," said Augustus, looking at her directly, "I want you to tell me some things that you enjoyed today."

The Princess sighed. "You don't understand my condition, Augustus. There is nothing that I can recollect that brought me joy."

"There is no hurry, Your Highness. Just sit awhile and recollect your day. Surely there were some things that pleasured you."

Sitting on the stool by the doorway, Augustus could see that Naomi's handmaiden seemed quite interested in the Princess's response.

"It is of no use, Augustus. I have had a miserable day and there is no point pretending anything different."

"Can you not recall anything that gave you pleasure?"

The Princess shook her head.

"Take your time and recollect your day in detail," requested Augustus.

Naomi sat there impassively, obviously reliving her day. Eventually a small smile eased across her countenance.

"Well, there was something. My handmaiden, Asma, brought to me a young puppy. It was so loveable and so gentle. It licked me when I cuddled it."

Sitting at the back of the room, the hand maiden smiled and went on with her sewing.

"Ah, that is good," said Augustus. "Keep that image firmly in your mind. Let us take a few moments to relive it and savour the joy you experienced. I want you to concentrate on the pleasure you derived from the naïve love of Asma's puppy."

They sat silently for perhaps three or four minutes. The Princess smiled as she recollected the experience. Then Augustus continued, "Was there anything else?"

Tears welled up in the eyes of the Princess. "Oh Augustus, you asked me to enquire after the health of my father. When I did that, his gratitude was palpable. How can I ever repay his kindness? He has tried so hard to make me well. The hardest thing about my depression is that I know how much it makes him suffer."

"How did you respond to his sense of gratitude?"

"My heart swelled with love for him. For a moment I felt I was the most fortunate person on this earth."

"Good! I want you also to relive your response to that sense of gratitude your father displayed this morning. When you go to bed this evening, I want you to consciously recapture those precious moments. Savour again those happy thoughts. Two such recollections shall do for today. Will you do this?"

"Yes, Augustus. I will try to relive those lovely moments. And Augustus, when will I be ready for you to show me how to get to the special place you mentioned this morning? I so greatly desire to be happy."

"In good time, Your Highness. There is a lot to do to earn entry into that special place."

"When we met this morning, you told me that you were going to try to get me to see the world differently. How can this be so? There is just the world out there and I can see it as well as anyone."

"Well, Princess, you are mistaken. What we have to deal with, is not the real world, but our interpretation of it. We all mainly see the world differently because of the meaning we impart to it and its constituents."

Naomi shook her head. "I do not understand Augustus."

"We largely do commerce, not with the real world, but our perception of it. The world we have to deal with is a construct of our minds."

"Can each of us really interpret things so differently?"

"Yes indeed. One of the problems that afflict those in your condition is how your own self-concept gets between you and the world."

"What do you mean?"

"Well, Princess, it is almost as though we see the world through a pane of glass. Some of us can't see the world objectively because we are obsessed with trying to see our own reflections in the glass."

The Princess looked pensive. "I will need to give some thought to this."

She arose from the floor and beckoned to Asma. "Should I come again to you tomorrow morning?"

"Yes, Princess. That should be our routine now—a session each morning and a session each evening." Naomi nodded. She then returned to her chamber with the handmaiden walking with her.

When they reached the room, the Princess turned to Asma and said and said, "Will you sit with me a while before you retire?"

When not in the company of others, Naomi and Asma displayed the friendship that had started in their childhoods. Asma put her hand affectionately on Naomi's shoulder. "Of course, Naomi. What is it you wish to discuss?"

"You know I value your opinion. I just wondered what you think of Augustus?"

Asma paused before replying, "It is a little early to pass judgment— but to tell the truth, I like him. He seems humble, but wise. His compassion is evident. I may be relying too much on my intuition, but I trust him. Mind you, I think he is very determined."

She looked up at the Princess, "But knowing you as I do, he will need to be determined, persistent as well as wise if he is to succeed."

Naomi smiled at her old friend. "That's a little impertinent Asma— but I suspect you are right. But thank you for sharing your thoughts with me. I am beginning to trust him as well, but I sometimes wonder, in my state, if I can trust my judgment. I am glad you have confirmed my feelings on this. He has told my father he might take six months or more to deal with my problem. It would be dreadful if I had to put up with someone for so long if I did not trust them. Thank you Asma, I will retire now."

Meanwhile Augustus was sitting cross-legged on the floor of his bedchamber contemplating the outcomes of the day. He was determined that he should coax the Princess to view the world differently. Her question about how was it possible to interpret the world in different ways was a typical response from those who were yet to understand. He had put the same question to his Master Takygulpa Rinpoche. He smiled as he remembered his Master's response.

"Old Yan Zi was said to have owned a small dog called Sunshi that barked incessantly.

The goldsmith who was an upright and optimistic man would walk past his house every morning. 'Ah, little dog,' he would say 'it is good to hear you so chirpy and positive.'

The calligrapher who was always grumpy and pessimistic came soon after. 'Why you little cur,' he mumbled, 'always complaining.'

The teacher, renowned for his insatiable curiosity then followed. 'Sunshi,' he said admonishingly, 'always full of questions.'

Finally along came the Emperor's cook. He was a very portly man. He shook his head and exclaimed, 'Poor little dog—always hungry.'

The dog, on the other hand, just liked the sound of his own voice."

CHAPTER 11

"The deeper that sorrow carves into your being, the more
joy you can contain."

Kahlil Gibrain

The next morning Augustus arose and ate from the platter that had been brought again to his room. There was some time before he was due to meet again with the Princess and so he went for a walk in the palace gardens. He walked in awareness, observing the flowers, the shrubs and the trees. He stopped and sat on a bench under a shady tree and listened to the bird calls. He inhaled the sweet smells. He stopped and rubbed his hand on the trunk of a tree and closed his eyes to accentuate the conflicting sensual feelings of roughness and softness of the bark. He tarried a while by the pond and watched the colourful goldfish gracefully swim among the waterlillies. Stilled mind—heightened senses—at one with the world.

He then retired to the ante-room where he was to meet the Princess and commenced his meditation practice to prepare himself. When seeking to help others he had learnt that it was more about his being than his doing. His Masters had taught that equanimity was one of the four "Divine States" that adepts aspire to, along with loving kindness, compassion and sympathetic joy.

Augustus sat cross-legged on the floor meditating. After thirty minutes or so, the Princess appeared. Again her face mirrored her distress. As they approached Asma again signified that she would wait by the door and do her needlework.

"Good morning, Naomi," said Augustus with a magnanimous smile.

Naomi pouted sulkily at Augustus. "It has not been a good morning," Augustus. "I have not slept well and I feel poorly."

"How is your father this morning?"

"Damn you, Augustus! Do you not care how I am? Why are you obsessed with the well-being of my father?"

Augustus responded gently, "If you are so greatly concerned about yourself, may not your father be also so distressed? Maybe also, if you learnt to be more concerned for your father you might not dwell so miserably on yourself."

She spun angrily on her heel and stormed off. In a little while she returned. Her anger had obviously dissipated. "He is well," Naomi responded. "He caressed me and thanked me for my concern," she continued. Then she wept.

"It seems to me," said Augustus, "that you are not in a state of mind where we can do anything constructive together. Let us wait now, and with your indulgence we can meet again this evening."

Naomi nodded and then ran off weeping. Asma arose from her seat and went to follow after. "No, no. Wait young lady—I would talk with you," said Augustus. The handmaiden stopped and turned to face the little Buddhist.

"If I am to help your mistress, it would be useful for me to know a little more about her. Can you help me with this?"

"Perhaps—what is it that you would know?"

"When Naomi is distressed by her condition, what happens?"

"Well, generally she retires to her bedchamber. She lies in bed and sporadically sleeps. She seems so full of lassitude that it is difficult, if not impossible, to get her to do anything."

"And what do you and the others do?"

"I generally sit by her bedside and hold her hand and try to console her. Her father also spends a great deal of time with her trying to cajole her out of her sad condition."

"Can I ask you not to encourage her distressing behaviour? When she gets distressed, care for her by all means but don't dote on her. However, when she is in good spirits, be extra nice to her then. It will help to reinforce the behaviours we want in her.'

She nodded. "I can see the sense in that, but it is difficult not to try and cheer her up."

Augustus smiled and Asma could see his compassion. "Sometimes," he said, "we have to suffer in the short term for our long term benefit. It is the paradoxical nature of humanity that sometimes suffering is necessary for great achievement. A mother suffers pain in giving birth to a wonderful child. An athlete suffers pain in his most glorious attainments. A warrior suffers in vanquishing his foe. The Buddha taught us that suffering is the natural outcome of the human condition. That is not to say that we should glorify our suffering. But we should accept our suffering and learn from it. The princess's condition is a complex one and only she can defeat it. It often requires that suffering should occur unmediated by the solicitations of others before there is the will to confront such a condition. This prison that she has constructed shields her from some of the anguish of the world but magnifies her own sense of unworthiness. It is only when she can appreciate that this self-inflicted, self-absorbed suffering may be worse than what confronting the world requires, then she may give pause to re-evaluate how she views the world."

"It will be hard for me not to try to console the Princess, but if it is to be helpful for her I will do my best."

"Thank you, Asma. And don't get disheartened. It takes a long time to change behaviours and there will inevitably be setbacks."

During the day Augustus walked into the city of Yolanpur. He remembered the bazaar with its intrigue and the commerce. But this time he passed quickly through the bazaar and into the city itself. He was dismayed to find that there was great poverty. On the outskirts of town the poor suffered in their hovels. He saw the children begging and the worn faces of the mothers attested to their hardship. Many of the children showed obvious signs of malnourishment. He was distressed by the contorted figures of the lame and infirm. This experience was quite a jolt after his cloistered time of being pampered in the palace.

Augustus returned to the palace in the late afternoon. He sat for a while in the lush surrounds of the garden and listened to the sounds of the water gurgling into the pool and the birds singing in the trees and undergrowth. His heart was full of compassion for those unfortunates that he had seen earlier. Perhaps he might find a way to ease their pain.

As evening fell, he found himself again in the ante-room wondering whether the Princess would appear. He meditated calmly for a time and then was interrupted by the approach of the Princess's hand-maiden Asma.

"Good evening, Asma. How goes your mistress?"

Asma looked a little flustered. "She has retired to her bed and won't get out. She asked me to tell you that she was too distressed to come to you. She said if you wished to speak to her this evening you must come to her."

The Buddhist sighed and shook his head. "Please relay to her this message—I will wait a while this evening and if she does not come, I will continue to come to this room at the appointed times and I will resume discourse with her when she is ready."

"She will not like your terms."

"I suspect not—but those are my terms."

Asma returned to the Princess's bedchamber and Augustus resumed his practice. Perhaps a half hour later, Augustus became aware of footsteps on the tiled floor. He looked up to see the Princess enter the ante-room with her handmaiden close behind. She strode purposefully towards the Buddhist. It was not sadness that clouded her face but a steely anger.

Augustus smiled benignly at the approaching figure. "Good evening, Princess. I am pleased that you saw fit to join me."

"Well I am not pleased that you have compelled me to arise from my sickbed to come here."

"Oh no, my Lady. I have not compelled you to do anything; nor would I be so presumptuous. Tell me why did you come?"

"I came because I promised my father I would work with you—but that was before I realised how heartless you are. You don't care for my welfare at all."

"Well, it may appear that way to you, Princess, but I would not have come all this way to work with you if I did not care for your condition."

"Hah, if you are so concerned about me, why is it that you never ask about my well-being."

"You may not want to hear this, my Lady, but I do not ask after your well-being because I think you are already unduly concerned with it, and I don't want to encourage you to be so self-obsessed."

Naomi drew in her breath. "How dare you? You are implying that my condition is caused because I am self-obsessed? I do not wish to be like this. I would much prefer to be otherwise. Yet you are insinuating I am responsible for my own suffering. Are you suggesting that I manufacture my condition—that I do it on purpose?"

"Not consciously, not deliberately. You readily admitted to me the other day that the cause of your discomfiture was your self criticism and self denigration. That occurs through no fault of your own. I am trying to divert your attention from yourself. A very wise man has told me that in order to achieve equanimity people must first know themselves, then accept themselves, and lastly, but most importantly, forget themselves."

Naomi shook her head. "This is difficult stuff indeed. How can I possibly accept myself when I know I am so unworthy? How can I accept that I should have this exalted position, a Princess no less, when I am so flawed and imperfect? It is my imperfections, my unworthiness that always dominates my mind. This is my lot and it shall always be so."

Augustus nodded. "It is the nature of your condition that you should believe thus. I could try to argue with you that you are a competent person; that you have no more faults than anyone else; that your imperfections are not just a result of your personal shortcomings but are also the products of your circumstances and the failures of others; but you are in no state to have such a rational debate. Come, if you want to progress with me let us resume our practice."

Reluctantly at first, Naomi was led into meditation. But soon there was a lightening of her features as though a weight had been removed from her shoulders. After a time, Augustus said, "Now come slowly to me. Be aware of your environment. Stretch your limbs and notice my voice. Open your eyes and reengage with the world."

The Princess had been greatly relieved by her meditation and had put aside her dysfunctional thoughts. Consequently it was with some reluctance she heeded Augustus's words.

"Now tell me," insisted Augustus, "What has happened to you today that has caused you joy?"

As before, the Princess was greatly affronted by this. "Do you not understand," she sobbed, "that in my condition there is nothing that could be described in the least way pleasant. There is no joy—only suffering and despair."

"Perhaps," said Augustus, "but think a little while longer."

This raised the ire of the Princess considerably. "Have you no understanding at all of my condition. I left you this morning in such despair I could not move from my bed."

"And what happened then, Princess?"

"I cried and cried. I was so distraught I could not even raise myself."

"And what happened then Princess?"

"Nothing! Nothing! I lay there in the depths of despair. There was nothing I could do."

"But what happened then, Princess."

"I was so distraught that finally my father came to try and console me." Her face softened. "He is so concerned for me. Even though I was greatly distraught, I appreciated his attention." She paused, remembering the moment. "I am so fortunate to have someone who loves me so."

Augustus said nothing but looked steadfastly at Naomi. After a long while she looked up and returned his gaze. Then she wept. "Yes, she said, amid her tears, "Yes that brought me joy."

"Does your father come to you often?"

"No, he is so busy with affairs of state that I do not see a lot of him. But he is a loving father and if he knows I am in distress, he always comes to me."

Augustus nodded. "That is enough for now. Let us meditate together again a little. When you retire I want you to relive the positive feelings you had when your father was with you. Will you do this?"

She sat awhile in thought and finally nodded her head. "But when are you going to address the underlying causes of my despair?"

"Be patient with me, Princess. I am not promising miracles but I am putting together a framework where you, yourself, will solve your problem—where you, yourself, will modify your behaviour in a positive way if you choose to."

Naomi didn't respond but took up her meditation position and resumed her practice. After a time she looked up again. "Augustus is there really a place where I can find peace? Have you misled me about this special place you talk about?"

"Oh no, Princess! There is such a place. But it is not a place of easy access. You have to be prepared, and ready to enter there. You need to have absorbed the lessons I have tried to teach you. When you have done that, entry into this special place will be easy."

"Oh I do hope so," she said. "I so long to be there."

CHAPTER 12

"The truth is that our finest moments are most likely
to occur when we are feeling deeply uncomfortable,
unhappy, or unfulfilled. For it is only in such moments,
propelled by our discomfort, that we are likely to step
out of our ruts and start searching for different ways or
truer answers."

M Scott Peck

The next morning, after his ablutions and breakfast, Augustus went to seek out the Grand Vizier. When he found him he said, "Abdullah, may I have word with you?" He had spoken frequently to Abdullah because the Sultan had asked the Grand Vizier to monitor progress in Augustus's endeavour and they were comfortable in each other's company and had learnt to trust each other.

"Of course, Augustus."

"Would you be able to arrange for me to see the Sultan, alone?"

A look of mild surprise came over the countenance of the Grand Vizier—but then he nodded. "I will try to arrange this. When do you wish to speak to him?"

"As soon as possible, please Abdullah."

"How is it going with the Princess?"

"We have made some preliminary progress—but it will take a while before I am able to engage the real underpinnings of her distress. But it would be useful if I could talk to her father."

"I will do what I can. Where will you be this morning?"

"I will retire now to my room and then a little later wait for the Princess in the ante-chamber."

"Very well; I will try to see the Sultan now."

So saying, he turned and strode off purposefully towards the throne room where the Sultan would customarily be attending to the matters of the day with his advisers.

After a while the Grand Vizier appeared at Augustus's door. He knocked and Augustus bade him enter. "You are in luck! The Sultan was scheduled to meet with the Prince of Urbhadzan this morning, but the Prince has sent an emissary to say he has been taken ill. Come quickly and you will have his full attention."

Augustus and Abdullah hurried from Augustus's room to the throne room. When they arrived there was no one there except the Sultan. Augustus looked to the right and to the left and was surprised that the only people in sight were a few of the Sultan's bodyguards posted by the entrances to the voluminous room and they were some distance away, out of earshot.

The Sultan seemed weary. He looked at Augustus and said, "You wanted to see me? I suspect it is about my daughter, is it not?"

"Yes it is," commented Augustus.

"You have been working with my daughter for some time and I find that she is alternately joyful and despairing. It is almost a month since we met and I asked you to report back after a month. Is that your purpose today?"

"Well, no sire. I have come to ask your assistance."

"What is it that you want? Are you to tell me you are not succeeding and you want to be done with my daughter?"

The Sultan's voice reflected a little anger. But then he added more plaintively, "Can you not find a path for her that would lead her to equanimity?"

"Well," replied Augustus, "I suspect I can. There is no easy solution to her condition. I have warned you it might take a considerable period of time."

Then to assure the Sultan he said, "We are making some progress—but if we are to further the Princess's healing there are some processes that you can help me with."

"And what are they?" demanded the Sultan.

"To begin with," explained Augustus, "when the Princess falls into what you call depression, do not encourage her."

"What do you mean?" asked the Sultan. "When my daughter is so distressed then of course it is my natural instinct to console her."

"With all due respect, Sultan, might I ask that you refrain from that response. Your daughter greatly desires your attention. It would help us considerably in rectifying her disorder if you gave her such attention when she was positive and in a good mood. It would help my intervention immensely if you could reward her with your affection when she was happy and positive rather than when she was depressed and negative."

The Sultan frowned. "You don't mean that I should ignore her when she is depressed?"

"No, don't ignore her. But if you can, don't reinforce her depression by your solicitude. Don't focus on her and her condition. Talk about other things that may interest her. Avoid any discourse that might make her feel sorry for herself."

The Sultan thought for a while. "This will be difficult but I will try. But tell me, will this make her better?"

"Perhaps not," said Augustus, "but it might provide me a space where I can show her how to heal herself."

"I am disappointed Augustus, because she initially showed some signs of improvement from your ministrations, but yesterday she fell back into her lassitude and suffering."

"I have told you, Your Highness, that this is not an easy journey. There is no guarantee of success and if I do succeed it will take some time. We are dealing with behaviours that have developed over many years. It would be foolish to believe we could displace them quickly. When she reverts to her old ways, it is her way of avoiding reality. It is a technique she has learnt unconsciously and it works for her in keeping the world at bay and it is reinforced when those that care for her shower her with attention."

"At least you are honest with me—not like those other charlatans that promised the world but delivered nothing."

"Just remember, that when she is as you would want her to be, lavish your attention on her. The Princess says that what you call her depression is a prison. It is a prison she feels she can't escape from. But then she misunderstands the nature of the prison. She herself constructed it. But it is not to keep her in—it is to keep the world out. What you call depression is the Princess's coping mechanism to keep the perceived distress of her world under control. She has constructed this prison and she has the capacity to deconstruct it. Do not reward her for retiring into the cloistered space of her prison walls. Reward her for every tentative step she makes to move outside her cell."

The Sultan nodded. "I can see the sense in your strategy and I will try to help, but I confess it will not be easy."

"That is all I ask", said Augustus who then took his leave.

As they walked back to his quarters, the Grand Vizier said, "That was a bold move, confronting the Princess's father in that way."

"It was necessary," replied Augustus. "He has an important part to play."

CHAPTER 13

Because the eye gazes but can catch no glimpse of it,
It is called elusive.
Because the ear listens but cannot hear it,
It is called rarefied.
Because the hand feels for it but cannot find it,
It is called infinitesimal.

                                        Lao Tzu

Augustus and the Grand Vizier sat on a bench in the palace gardens. The two had become friends and Abdullah often sought out Augustus in the evenings. He admired Augustus's intellect and they shared stimulating conversation.

Abdullah mused, "Augustus you are a Buddhist and as I understand it, devoted to the cause of the amelioration of suffering. Why is it the lot of humans to have to deal with pain and suffering? Here we are living with the most powerful man in this country—but he suffers. And as much as he has tried to alleviate it, his beloved daughter suffers also."

Augustus remembering a lesson from his teacher, Takygulpa Rinpoche, replied, "When you understand who you really, really are, then there is no pain and suffering. It is true that your body may suffer; it is true that your mind may suffer; but at the level of the Witness, there is no suffering. Our hearts go out to those who are deceived and identify themselves with mind and body, but underneath it all, we know all is well."

His companion looked quizzically at him. "What is this Witness you talk about?" [2]

"It is not easy to explain. The Witness is an outcome of our consciousness."

"In common with all physical life on the planet, we humans have a body. From our body we derive physical needs. If we don't satisfy our physical needs we die—physically. Fulfilment of our physical needs allows us to survive."

"In common with all animals on the planet, we humans have a brain. Through the cognitive processes of our brains we are able to discern the world and make decisions. From this mental capacity comes our second set of needs, one that we share with all the animals of the world. The second set of needs are our social needs. Like all animals, we have the capacity to be aware of our outer world and to respond to it through the processes of thinking, feeling, and decision making. Like all animals we are intimately connected through strong emotional bonds to our fellow creatures, particularly those of our own species and those close to us. If we do not find reasonable satisfaction for our social needs we die—emotionally (and sometimes even physically). Fulfilment of our social needs allows us to cope emotionally."

"The third set of needs are spiritual needs—needs for meaning, the uniquely human needs. If we are unable to meet our spiritual needs and fail to find meaning in our lives we die—spiritually (and sometimes socially and physically). Fulfilment of our spiritual needs and gaining a sense of personal worth through finding meaning and purpose in our lives is needed if we are going to experience our full humanity. Meeting these needs provides a transcendent sense of well-being, i.e. a sense of well being that transcends the condition of our immediate circumstances."

"The question we now ask is, 'What is this other dimension of our humanity that leads to this third set of needs, the uniquely human needs that differentiate us from other animals?' To understand this we must explore the nature of consciousness."

---

[2]   Much of the material for this chapter is derived from Dr Phil Harker's Tripartite Model of Humanity

"Consciousness is the faculty that differentiates humans from other animals. Human beings are not only aware, as indeed all animals are, but as far as we can tell we are the only animal that is aware of its awareness. There is no doubt that other animals are aware of their exterior worlds. Without such awareness they would not survive. In dealing with this outside world all animals make decisions. But the defining characteristic of Humanity is that not only are we aware of the outside world and make decisions about it in our day to day discourse with the world, but that all these processes are carried out in the theatre of our awareness."

"Because of our consciousness then, we are aware of some of the internal processes of our mind. We thus create the construct of an 'interior' world. The building blocks of this construction are our personal thoughts, feelings and temporal experience. And it is the condition of this internal world that has the greatest impact on our sense of well-being."

He paused to see whether Abdullah had taken all this in. His companion nodded, "Please go on."

"If you consider a conscious being, like you and I, there are three elements that constitute it. As we saw earlier there is a body and a mind. But what is it that allows us to 'watch' the theatre of mind, to be aware of our thoughts, our daydreams, and the various cogitations of mind? In my tradition, we call this faculty the Witness."

"Then," asked his companion, "why is it I am not aware of this faculty?"

"It is because you have nothing with which to be aware of it. Your mind is able to perceive your body and the Witness perceives your mind. And as you can see there is a hierarchy here and each level can see the level below. But there is nothing with which to be aware of the Witness. We know it is there by inference only. The sages ask, 'Can an eye see itself or can a knife cut itself?' No, and in this manner the Witness can not be aware of itself."

"But you say this is the highest level in the hierarchy? Does that mean it is the most important?"

"Yes indeed, because you see this is your essential self, who you really are. You are not your body because your body changes in many ways both because of environmental conditions and the inevitable process of aging. You are not your mind because the thoughts that come into awareness are constantly changing as well. It is the Witness that gives us an enduring sense of self because only it remains constant."

"But how does this have any bearing on our propensity to suffer?"

"Augustus continued, "The problem is that most of us don't know who we really are. Most of us identify with this body and this mind. Both of which are vulnerable. You do not suffer. Only the person you imagine yourself to be suffers. Let me try to illustrate this with a Zen parable."

"There was a master who taught his disciples that the entire world is an illusion and it was folly to become attached to an illusion. The master had an only son and through some misfortune the son was killed. A disciple went to the master and found him weeping. 'Why do you weep?' asked the disciple. 'After all, the world and everything in it is an illusion.' 'Ah yes,' agreed the master, 'but to lose an only son is the cruellest of all illusions.'"

"It is hard to put aside those emotional attachments we have. It seems part of the human condition to hang on to them. But the enlightened understand that—although all the earthly manifestations may seem to point to the contrary—all is well. So you see, although I might cling to some notions of injustices and suffering, in the final analysis there is no injustice and there is no suffering for all is well."

"In the end, it comes back to our awareness; how we perceive the world. Our wellbeing then depends not so much on what we do, but who we are. Even more so, it depends on who we think we are. When we identify with the transient and vulnerable we are fearful. When we identify with the true substance of our humanity we are content. Don't worry about the external circumstances, my friend. There may be wars and difficulties, injustices and insults, but once you come to know who you really are, all is well."

"Does that mean," asked the Grand Vizier, "that one who is enlightened will pay no heed to the suffering of others? Does it mean, therefore, that the enlightened one can deal with others however he pleases?"

"He can *always* do as he pleases," replied Augustus. "Though, of course, someone who knows his life is one with all and will have no inclination to do harm to another, for that would not 'please' him. Furthermore, his understanding of the real needs of others will inform him as to when it is appropriate to help and when it would be harmful to help."

"Are you suggesting that it is sometimes harmful to help others?" responded Abdullah incredulously.

Augustus nodded. "Look at the ruination that help has caused to so many people and so many countries around the world. This is because it sometimes reinforces their belief that they are helpless. Often, at times, the mind is so focussed on obtaining such help it is blinded to other options. There is a paradox here. The enlightened one seeks an end to suffering not merely the alleviation of suffering. And sometimes it is suffering itself that finally causes us to act to end suffering. It is the burden of the unbearable that goads us to a final resolution. The temporary amelioration of suffering removes the spur to that final solution."

"This is hard to accept," said the Grand Vizier, shaking his head. "So, based on this approach, you might just leave a person to die even if you were in an immediate position to help."

"No, of course not," said Augustus with an indulgent smile. "A person who loves will do what any peaceful, loving person would do if the giving of help was truly beneficial and within the sphere of their influence. However, you must understand that being enlightened does not prescribe how an individual should act. Enlightenment gives them a way of seeing the world stripped of illusions. Because they have learnt not to identify with their mind and their body, they can put aside fear. From this detached point of view they are more likely to be able to discern when help is truly beneficial and when it is not. Sometimes, help merely reinforces long-term suffering. Witness the amount of discontent that people experience when they see others possessing more than they do. Then there arises an unhelpful desire to acquire more. Helping such a pursuit would not be useful, because there is no end to it. Contentment will never be achieved that way."

"You have given me much to contemplate tonight my friend. But I must go now. Let's talk again soon."

Augustus smiled. "I look forward to it."

CHAPTER 14

"In short, self-absorption in all its forms kills empathy,
let alone compassion. When we focus on ourselves, our
world contracts as our problems and preoccupations loom
large. But when we focus on others, our world expands.
Our own problems drift to the periphery of the mind
and so seem smaller, and we increase our capacity for
connection—or compassionate action."

Daniel Goleman

The days went by and Augustus and Naomi fell into an easy routine. She
would come to him in the morning and he would always ask after her
father. She took more and more interest in her father and would relate
to Augustus not only his state of health but also his appointments for the
day and the decisions he had to make. Then they would meditate.

In the evenings they would try to reclaim the joy of the good things
that had happened and relive the special moments in Naomi's life.

Her meditation practice grew more proficient and she came to enjoy
these times. She found serenity in those hours she spent with her mind
stilled. After a time, she seemed to take more and more of that serenity
into her day to day life.

Some weeks went by without incident. Then one evening Augustus
asked the Princess to relive the most joyful events of her day. She said,
"Augustus it has been a lovely day! It has been a long time since I
enjoyed myself so."

Augustus smiled. It was unusual for the Princess to give such a positive response. This was a significant statement from the Princess. Augustus knew that sufferers of depression are said to be anhedonic—that is not able to experience pleasure. For her to be so positive about her experiences was a very hopeful sign.

"Well to begin with when I got out of bed this morning, Asma was there with a beautiful bouquet of flowers. I said, 'Asma, they are so beautiful. Why have you brought them to me?' And Asma, may Muhammad bless her, said, 'My lady you have been such a joy to be with these last few weeks, I just wanted to show my appreciation.' I was so moved I wept."

"Asma is surely a treasure for you," nodded Augustus. "And what else happened."

"Well Augustus, I went to my father to enquire after his well-being, and he said, 'Naomi, my love now that you seem more cheerful, I would like to spend more time with you. Would you like to ride in the countryside with me this afternoon?' I was so overjoyed that of course I agreed. It is many years since my father indulged me thus. And we had such a lovely time. He on his black stallion and I on my little white mare, we rode out into the countryside. And after we had gone well beyond the city, where there was no sign of human habitation at all, we stopped by a lovely little stream and we just talked for an hour or so. It has been so long since I have had that sort of time with my father. And he said that he enjoyed our outing so much that he would like to ride with me every week! Oh, Augustus, how generous he is—with all his affairs of state he wants to put aside some time for me. I am so lucky to have such a loving father."

"You are indeed Princess. But he is fortunate as well to have such a loving daughter. Can I ask you as always to relive these moments when you retire. Savour them again. These are precious moments not to be put lightly aside. Relive them before you sleep and your repose will be sweet."

"There is no need to berate me to relive my joys today, Augustus. Even without your counsel I am sure I would have done so, and indeed I have already relived them many times."

"Savour every moment of your satisfaction, Princess!"

Following this exchange, Augustus and the Princess sat together in the lotus position and pursued the meditative processes in which Augustus had been schooling Naomi for these last few months.

The next day, the Sultan sent for Augustus. "I want to thank you," he said, "for making such an improvement in the Princess's condition. Why, I went riding with her yesterday and she was a joy to be with."

"I am pleased, Your Highness, but I caution you not to be too optimistic. It is inevitable that there will be a relapse. I have not yet begun the most important phase of my instruction of her. We have used these devices of meditation and positive feedback to make a little space for me to put her happiness on a much firmer foundation. Just remember that whatever transpires give her most attention when her behaviour is as you'd want it to be."

The Sultan seemed a little nonplussed that Augustus was suggesting that Naomi's depression was only temporarily in abatement. Nevertheless, he nodded. "You seem to know what you are doing. How joyous I would be if Naomi could always be as she was with me yesterday."

"I suspect that it is unlikely that the Princess can always be that way, but I am sure that with patience we can ensure any relapses are infrequent and of shorter duration."

"Then that is all I could ask for. I have today, enjoyed the company of my daughter more than I have for many years. Please do not hesitate to come to me if there is any way I can help your progress."

"Thank you Your Highness. I rely on your support and you have been most helpful already." Augustus then retired.

It was evening now and he walked through the palace back to his bedchamber. Whilst he was deep in thought about how to proceed with Naomi, he was still very alert. As he approached his bedchamber he became aware of a soft scuffling noise coming from the room.

He approached stealthily. At the doorway he paused and peered into the semi-darkness of the unlit room. There at the rear of the room was a small figure searching through Augustus's meagre possessions. It was a young boy perhaps eleven or twelve years old. So engrossed was he in his activity that Augustus was able to approach quite close to him before the boy noticed that he was being observed. He gave a quick gasp and bolted towards the doorway. But Augustus was too quick and grabbed the boy's tunic.

"Let me go! Let me go!" the boy called shrilly.

"What were you doing?" Augustus asked.

The boy fell to the ground and sobbed. "I was trying to find some money for my mother. She has three children to support and no husband."

Augustus was concerned. "Why do you have no father?" he enquired.

"My father died two years ago. My mother has no income and no way to support her children. I know it is wrong to steal from others but I have no choice. My mother cannot survive, let alone support her children without some supplementary income. I do not want to be a thief but I know no other way of supporting my mother."

Augustus released his grip on the boy's tunic.

"I do not have much money," he said, "And unfortunately for you it is in a little purse attached to my belt."

"How were you able to get into the palace?" asked Augustus. "It is well-defended by guards and it would seem unlikely to me that you could make your way unencumbered into my room."

"I cannot tell you that sir, because that is the only skill I have that can enable me to bring sustenance to my mother and my siblings."

"What is your name, young man?"

"Oh, sir, I cannot tell you. If I tell you my name the Sultan will punish my mother for allowing me to steal from the palace."

"Well, my boy, I can assure you that if you cooperate with me, I will tell the Sultan nothing."

The youth looked up into Augustus's face and he could see his compassion. He burst into tears.

"I can not tell you Master. I can tell you nothing lest it harms my mother."

Augustus placed his arms around the lad and hugged him.

"I will do nothing to harm you or your mother. And although I don't have much I will give you a little money to take home to her."

He knelt down in front of the boy and asked him again, "Please tell me your name."

The lad looked into Augustus's face and again recognised the compassion in his visage. He looked down at his feet and seemed to think for a while. He hesitated and then responded. "Sir, I don't know why I trust you but I do. Will you swear solemnly not to take any action that might impact badly on my mother?"

"Do not concern yourself, young man. I won't do anything to harm you or your mother."

The boy looked Augustus directly in the eye and said, "It is against my better judgment, but there is something about you that makes me confident that you will keep your word. My name is Babak."

"Thank you," said Augustus. "And your two siblings are they boys or girls."

"I am the eldest and I have two younger sisters."

He seemed about to weep again. But he wiped his eyes and again looked up at Augustus. "My sisters are so beautiful and so loving, I must do what I can to support them."

"You are well-named young man."

"What do mean, sir?"

"I understand that Babak means 'little father' and that is what you seem to aspire to be."

The boy smiled.

Augustus withdrew a little leather bag from his tunic. "Let me see what I can find for you."

He withdrew three small gold coins and placed them in the boy's hand. The boy gasped.

"This is probably all I can afford right now."

The lad stood open-mouthed. Then after a time he seemed to recover his senses and responded, "Oh, sir that is so generous. And what are you called so that I might properly thank you and tell my mother of our benefactor."

"My name is Augustus."

The boy wrinkled his brow. "That is a strange name."

And then he quickly added, "Oh I am sorry Master—I meant no offence."

Augustus merely laughed.

"I am not offended. And it is truly a strange name for someone to have here. My name is derived from another tradition entirely. But don't worry about that."

Augustus bowed and his eyes twinkled. "How do you do, Babak."

The boy smiled. "I am very well now thank you."

Then the boy bowed. "And how do you do, Augustus?"

"I am happy to have found a little friend. But now let's get you out of here without incurring the wrath of the sentries."

The boy looked perplexed.

"How do you propose to do that?" he asked.

"Simple—I will just walk with you out the front door of the palace."

"But we will be in full view of the sentries," said Babak looking concerned.

"Well so we might—but I come and go a lot and I've been here now for some time so most of the sentries know me. They will most likely assume that somebody accompanying me is a legitimate visitor to the palace."

Together they exited Augustus's room. Babak was clearly concerned and his eyes went left and right in fear of being apprehended. But as they were leaving the corridor that led from Augustus's room they happened to come upon the Grand Vizier. Babak was terrified.

Abdullah greeted Augustus warmly.

"So how goes it Augustus. It must be time for us to have another philosophical chat. What are you doing later this evening?"

"I would like nothing more than to share your company, Abdullah."

"Good! I will come to your quarters when I am finished with the Sultan and we can resume our ongoing discussion."

Then Abdullah looked at Augustus's companion. "And who is this you have with you?" he enquired.

"It is just a young friend of mine. I'm trying to balance my social life you see. I have an old friend," he said nodding to the Grand Vizier, "And now I have a young friend." And thus saying he turned and smiled at Babak.

"I am pleased you know the boy, Augustus. But be careful with security of your possessions because I have heard there is a thief about. We suspect it must be a nimble young person who can scale the palace wall and squeeze in through a small aperture somewhere. You haven't lost anything have you—anything you might suspect as having been stolen?"

"No not at all," Augustus replied.

Abdullah looked at Babak. "You are not a thief are you young man?"

The boy's heart went into his mouth.

"You certainly look nimble and agile."

Augustus quickly responded. "Come Abdullah, leave the young fellow alone. He has enough problems. He has lost his father and lives in the poor part of the city with his mother and two sisters where they struggle to survive. He sought charity from me and I gave him a few coins."

The Grand Vizier was also a compassionate man and far wealthier than Augustus. But he was no fool. He suspected Augustus was shielding the boy.

He smiled at the lad. "I didn't mean to offend you, young man. Can I add a little to help?"

So saying, he pulled a little money bag from his robes and placed a half dozen coins in Babak's hand.

"Would you, young sir, be prepared to exchange this for what Augustus has given you? You see Augustus has great charity but little means—whereas I have a little charity but far greater means."

Babak was overwhelmed by this gesture and could merely nod his head. He reached into his tunic and gave Abdullah the coins Augustus had given him.

Abdullah in turn pressed the few coins into Augustus's hand and insisted he take them back.

"You are very generous, old friend, but surely you must appreciate three gold coins mean little to me who has few material needs."

"And six gold coins mean little to me, Augustus, because I have many of them. But this is not the most important issue."

He turned to Babak. "Young man you look fit and physically competent. Would you do a little work for the Sultan? There would of course be some payment."

The young man was bewildered. After a pause he finally asked, "What is it sir, that you would have me do?"

"Well at the rear of the palace the Sultan has an orchard. There are many varieties of fruit trees. The chief gardener is old and arthritic and finds it difficult to pick the fruit. Sometimes to properly harvest the fruit you have to climb the fruit trees and of course that is beyond him."

And then, with but the hint of an ironical smile, he continued, "I suspect that you might be good at climbing."

Babak didn't know what to say.

"You are very kind, Abdullah," said Augustus.

The Grand Vizier winked slyly at his Buddhist friend. "I just thought this might be a productive way to harness your young friend's talents and help him contribute to the upkeep of his family."

Babak had found his voice. He fell to the ground at the Grand Vizier's feet. "Oh thank you, sir. I would be more than happy to work in the Sultan's orchard."

"Very well young man—come and see me tomorrow and I will introduce you to the gardener. You may not think so but I am aware of the poverty in the city and I would like to help in what little way I can."

He then turned to Augustus. "I am pleased to have met your little friend Augustus, and I look forward to taking up our philosophical discussion later in the evening."

Augustus smiled at his friend. "I look forward to it also. Might I say you have been a great example of loving-kindness this day. I might have to make you an honorary Buddhist."

"No need Augustus! I don't aspire to your religion, but I do aspire to your altruism."

"Well you have surely demonstrated that!" said Augustus.

He then led the boy out of the palace. As he had predicted there were no challenges from the sentries. Outside the palace gates Augustus bade farewell to Babak. But Babak couldn't restrain himself. He placed his arms around the little Buddhist and hugged him which was a little disconcerting to Augustus.

"Oh thank you Augustus for what you have done for me tonight."

"Don't thank me, young man. It is the Grand Vizier you should thank. Not only has he given you money to help support your family but he has found you employment as well."

"But it would never have happened Augustus, if you hadn't forgiven me for trying to steal from you."

"You never need to steal from me Babak. I will always share with you what I have. But make a promise to me."

"What is that?"

"No more stealing. If you and your family are in need come and see me and I will try to help."

"I will not steal Augustus. With your friend's generosity we have sustenance enough for a considerable period now. When I went to the palace to steal I thought that its inhabitants were fair targets—they were people of means who seemed to me to have no concern for the poor. Well I have met two tonight who have proved my assumption wrong. So thank you so much. And now I can't wait to see my mother and tell her of my good fortune."

And so saying the boy turned and ran out into the night.

CHAPTER 15

"As long as anyone believes that his ideal and purpose is outside him, that it is above the clouds, in the past or in the future, he will go outside himself and seek fulfillment where it cannot be found. He will look for solutions and answers at every point except where they can be found— in himself."

Erich Fromm

It was now over three months since Augustus had begun his work with the Princess. The Princess had grown fond of him and could see that his efforts had improved her quality of life. The handmaiden, Asma, had played a part as well. She continued to reinforce the positive emotions of the Princess, as did the Sultan.

Then one morning Naomi asked, "What next, Augustus? I am reasonably competent at meditation. I have learnt how to do my affirmations every evening. Is that all there is?"

Augustus smiled. "No, Princess. There is much more to do yet. We have managed to give you some palliative care. By and large, you are coping much better. But we have yet to give you a platform for enduring happiness."

Naomi mused for a while and then said, "Sometimes I believe I have been striving for the wrong things. When I look back at my behaviour I see a dichotomy. I have either been trying to avoid the world by retreating to my prison or I have tried overly much to engage the world.

And that doesn't seem to have helped either. Perhaps you can explain something for me, Augustus?"

"I will try. What is it you wish to know?"

"In between my bouts of depression, I have led a very full life. One would think that that would be an antidote to becoming so self-obsessed as I concede I do when depressed.'

"Well, my lady, I suppose it is a matter of what your life is full of. Let me give you an example." And here Augustus walked to the table set up for an oncoming feast and picked up two goblets. The Princess looked on perplexed at this.

"Here, mind these," he said and marched off in the direction of the kitchen. He came back with some soap. Taking a knife off the table he shaved some of the soap into one goblet. He then seized a pitcher of water from off the table and poured a little into the goblet with the shaved soap and then filled up the other goblet. He took a spoon from off the table and vigorously whisked the contents of the goblet which held a little water and the soap flakes. Very soon he had generated a goblet full of frothy soap suds.

"This," he said, "is like your life. This goblet is full, but it is full of froth whipped up by my vigorous attention. Your life is equally full of diversions and past-times. Let us leave the goblet settle a while."

As they watched, the froth subsided and the goblet became only a quarter filled with its contents.

"So this is like your life. Unless you are continuously whipping up its contents with your temporary pleasures and diversions, it will soon subside. It has little substance at all."

He then pointed to the other goblet. "See, this one has not changed because its contents have substance. Occasionally the breeze may blow hard and generate a few ripples over the top, but underneath the bulk of its contents remain unmoved. When you fill your life with substance you will also be impervious to the environmental variations and you will be calm and content."

"And what," enquired the princess, "is the stuff of substance that I should seek to fill up the goblet of my life?"

"In general," replied the Buddhist, "there are two kinds. Let me try to explain."

"Every one of us has such qualities that when we use them we become engaged and engrossed. These are our particular strengths.

In such engagement we come to forget ourselves and the passage of time passes without our awareness. Such pursuits engage our whole being. It happens when the hunter approaches his prey. He is aware of everything—the rustle of the leaves, the scent of the woods, the caress of the breeze, the distant birdsongs—everything but himself. It may be the seamstress concentrating on the manufacture of a difficult garment, the potter trying to fashion the perfect piece, the mathematician struggling to find the proof of a theorem, the orator in front of the admiring crowd. There is some such pursuit for everyone. When we live a life that gives us ample opportunity to practice such strengths, have them tried and extended, we fill the goblet with substance. What is it that you do that so engages yourself?"

The princess looked down, obviously deep in thought. Then a small smile came fleetingly across her countenance. "I think for me it happens when I play music. In my youth I was taught to play the flute. When depressed I have often found it a relief to take time off by myself to play. I get engrossed in the music, particularly difficult passages and before I know it, hours have passed. When I am like this it is a relief to play—but I play for myself. I find it much more difficult when I am requested to play for an audience."

"That is because you are vulnerable when your sense of self is fragile. You then concern yourself with how others might view you and the slightest mistake you make is magnified in your mind to a perceived disaster. And, I suspect, when you are obsessed with how others might perceive you, your attention to the music wanes and you're more likely to make a mistake! Your concern about failing in front of an audience then becomes a self-fulfilling prophecy!"

The Princess sighed. "That is so true. But on those occasions when I am with my music and not with my audience, it is so uplifting!"

"Then it is important," rejoined Augustus, "for you to schedule such time into your daily life. Put aside some time every day to play your flute."

"But Augustus," said Naomi, "I am a princess and I have obligations. Would it not seem that I was indulging myself if I were to devote some hours a day to my music?"

Augustus smiled. "Well some might think so; but this will improve your effectiveness as a human being and will actually improve your ability to make a contribution to your society. It often takes courage to do the things you need to do because others often have other plans for you! But you should have no concern about taking up your music. If we can restore your zest for life, you will be more productive and more effective in everything you do. It is strange that if you were an athlete you would immediately see the need to train your body. If you were a teacher you would not argue that you would have to train your mind. Well, let me make it clear, to be a fully functioning human being you need to train your spirit. Hopefully that is what playing your music will do to you."

"If you suppress your need to utilise these special strengths, play it safe and conform to the desires of others, then something essential in you is lost. But if you follow this internal call, you enhance your psychological robustness and capture a joy that will not be available from most other pursuits. This is a life-affirming decision for you."

"And that brings us to consider the second kind of activity which will help you to add substance to your goblet of life."

"And what might that be?" enquired the princess.

"It is the pursuit of meaning. This is an essential characteristic of human beings. The thing that differentiates us from other animals is that we are self-aware. Because of this we not only have to deal with a world 'out there,'" and Augustus waved his arm expansively in front of himself, "but we have also to deal with a world 'in here', an internal world," and Augustus tapped his head.

"Once it is has become our lot not just to take our place in the world, but to observe our being in the world, it is natural then to ask 'What are we here for? What is the purpose of my life?' We seem then to have a need to find a sense of meaning and purpose in our lives. These are our spiritual needs. This manifests itself in a motivation to devote ourselves to something that is bigger than ourselves. We need to make a difference. We need to contribute to a cause that is beyond our self-serving egos."

"I am sure you are right, Augustus. I have always had a desire to make a contribution, to help others, to improve our society. My father has been a great example in that regard. He is generous and kind. And he has always worked to ensure that the entire citizenship of his suzerainty would profit from his leadership."

"He is a good example for you then, Princess. But one thing at a time. Let us first ensure that you can put music back into your life before we take another step to engage your spiritual needs."

"Then let us begin to empty the froth from my goblet and try to fill it with some of your stuff of substance," Naomi offered. Augustus smiled. The Princess's positive response gave him optimism that they might be able to further enhance her psychological robustness.

"Very well then. From tomorrow you will bring your flute and after meditation we will devote an hour to playing."

Naomi then looked inquiringly at Augustus. "What of you Augustus? What brings meaning onto your life?"

The little man smiled. "There are two things my lady. Firstly helping to reduce the impact of suffering is important to me. As part of that I get particular fulfillment from seeing others benefit from having more appropriate ways of viewing the world."

The Princess returned his smile. "As indeed you seem to be succeeding in doing for me. But what else?"

"The other thing My Lady, is that I wish to understand humanity as well as I can. You see my Buddhism is informed by a thousand years of contemplation and study of the human mind. That is of particular interest to me."

Naomi nodded thoughtfully. It was a thought she stored away in her own mind. Maybe at some time in the future the roles may be reversed and she could in fact help Augustus.

She returned to the present. "So tomorrow I will bring my flute. I am looking forward to that."

Augustus beamed. "Indeed your lady, I am as well!"

So it was that the Princess resumed her playing. She was indeed very proficient. After a time, members from the palace household would come and stand outside the door just to listen. The Sultan, heard of her morning exercises and went to hear for himself. He just stood outside the door and beamed.

One day, after Naomi had played beautifully for her assigned hour, there came a spontaneous burst of applause from outside the door. Augustus, who had been unaware of the Princess's audience, hurried to the door to chase them away. But the Princess, just laughed and said, "Let them be, Augustus. If I can put a few moments of joy into their lives, so be it." Augustus was greatly heartened by this response. Again it was a sign that the Princess's robustness had increased.

When he went for his now weekly ride with the Princess, the Sultan told her how proud he was of her and how much he enjoyed her playing. He asked her would she like to play sometimes with the court musicians. Naomi agreed. Because her sense of self was now much more steadfast, she got great satisfaction from playing in the little ensemble. On occasions she played with them also in the court for visiting heads of state. As she became more confident, the mastery of her music began to mean much more to her than her concerns of approbation from her audience.

Thus the confidence and the optimism of Naomi seemed to grow and flourish.

CHAPTER 16

"Character cannot be developed in ease and quiet. Only
through experience of trial and suffering can the soul
be strengthened, vision cleared, ambition inspired, and
success achieved."

Helen Keller

All was quiet. Except for muffled sounds of activity coming from
somewhere more remote in the palace and the barely audible but pleasant
sounds of birdcalls drifting in from the palace garden. His concentration
on his breathing merely heightened Augustus's awareness. When he
heard the footsteps approaching he knew immediately it was Naomi.
But he also knew something was wrong. The lightness of her step that
had become so familiar in these last few weeks was gone.

The Princess entered the room dragging her flute by her side and
her cheeks were wet with tears. She slowly sat down on a cushion in
front of the Buddhist and assumed her meditation position. Augustus
nodded at her but said nothing. The Princess began her meditation
practice. After a while she seemed to regain her composure. Despite her
troubled mind, the continuous practice ensured she could easily engage
herself in meditation. After her usual routine she roused herself from
meditation and looked toward the little Buddhist. His eyes, as ever, were
full of compassion, but still he said nothing. Finally Naomi blurted out,
"Augustus, I have to talk—I've had a relapse."

"After the music," came the reply.

"But I have finished my practice."

"Your music is now as much your practice as your meditation. Please play."

The young woman sighed and then taking up her instrument, played a doleful air.

When she had finished, Augustus nodded and said, "Good, now play some more." Then, without stopping, Naomi played for a full half-hour. She played difficult pieces with rippling arpeggios, with subtle key changes and dramatic leaps.

"Enough," said Augustus at the end. "That was beautiful. Now tell me what you want to talk about.

"I have regressed. I woke up this morning in a pall of despair. And I've had such a lovely few weeks. I can not remember being so happy. Now it is all gone. Now I am back to where I started."

"But you are not, Princess," said Augustus.

"What do you mean?"

"You are here with me. You have meditated and practiced your flute. You have done something positive. You are not lying in bed feeling sorry for yourself."

"But I am not happy and I have experienced so much happiness lately that I had an expectation that it would ever continue thus."

"Then you are mistaken. Our emotions come and go and even the wisest sage will have his equanimity challenged. Is there any land where the sky is forever blue? Is there any tree that flowers continuously? Is there a river that runs placidly in all its reaches? Is there a sea with no tides? This is the nature of things, a reflection of the impermanence and the constant change that underpins the universe. That is why the Buddha taught that we should become attached to nothing, not even happiness. The techniques we have learnt together will help you deal with your unhappiness and reduce the frequency of its occurrence, but do not believe it is possible to live forever happily."

"I thought my meditation practice would help me stay happy."

"Your meditation practice helps in many ways, but there are two outcomes that are particularly helpful. Firstly it makes you more aware. When the mind is stilled you become aware of your emotional state. Secondly, being thus aware of your emotion, you can detach yourself from it. When I first met you, you were unaware emotionally because your emotions dominated and overwhelmed you. You did not notice your despair so much as identified with it. You could not notice objectively because in many ways you *were* your despair. Here, come outside awhile with me."

Intrigued, Naomi followed the little Buddhist out into the garden.

"Look up and tell me what you see."

"Why, I see a blue sky with some clouds scurrying across it."

"Consider that lovely blue sky as a metaphor for your true self. See how sometimes the clouds partly obscure it. Those clouds are your thoughts and your emotions. But we know from our vantage point that the clouds are not the sky. From the awareness of meditation you will be able to see that neither your thoughts nor your emotions are your true self. Because we are detached from the clouds, when we look up we can say, 'Look, there is a cloud beginning to impinge on the sky.' When we come to learn detachment from our thoughts and our emotions, we can look inwards and say, 'Look here comes some despair which is impinging on my true self.' We know, just as with the clouds, we can patiently observe its passage, not identifying with it, and that soon enough it will be gone. It seems to me that you are beginning to learn this lesson otherwise you would still be in bed crying, acting out your despair and not dealing constructively with it."

"Why is it Augustus, that we can not lock our happiness away so securely that it can not be sullied?"

"It is the way of the world, Naomi. And yet we are each different. Some of us are born with a greater propensity for sorrow than others. It comes from our parents and our ancestors. Was your mother disposed to sorrow and pessimism?"

The Princess looked down at the ground. "Yes," she replied. "My mother was often full of despair. She seemed often to interpret things in a very pessimistic way."

"It is like our metaphor of the clouds. Some countries have lots of days with cloudy skies. I have heard in some countries there are tropical rainforests where it rains almost every day. And there are countries, we know, that are dominated by deserts where months or years can pass without a cloud being seen. It is an outcome of the natural diversity that pervades the earth. Similarly, people vary. Some are born with positive and optimistic dispositions and others with more negative and pessimistic dispositions. But even those who are the most positive among us are not immune from despair. They encounter it less frequently and they have better ways of innately coping with it. People with your disposition encounter despair more frequently but the problem is magnified because you have poor strategies for coping with it. In our practice we will try to learn strategies to make your episodes of sadness less frequent but perhaps more importantly, we will learn how to manage those episodes more effectively. Even now, because you have become engaged with your music, your thoughts of self have waned and your sadness is ebbing. Is that not true?"

A fleeting smile stole across her face. Then Naomi nodde,. "That is true."

She shook her head, musing to herself.

"What is it Princess?" Augustus enquired.

The Princess looked at the little Buddhist and enquired, "You have told me, Augustus, that we each have different worldviews and because we see the world differently we respond to the world differently."

"Yes—that is so Princess."

"But how can these view points be so different?"

"Some of us are inwardly focused and fearful and as a result we can't see very far. We are always looking for those things that we believe are threatening us. We can't see beyond the next slight or insult. We see the world as a threatening place. Others that are more at ease with themselves are able to see the world more benignly. To them the world is a more congenial place and they are more likely to be at one with their world."

"Let me give you an example. Consider a green ant living with its colony in a mangrove tree. The ant is gnawing at the edge of a leaf. All of a sudden, a gust of wind arises and breaks the leaf from its branch. The leaf, with the ant clinging grimly to it, tumbles down into the water. The tide is running out and the leaf is whirled around by the eddies formed where the mangrove roots meet the water. The ant is thrust violently about and hangs on for grim death. Eventually the leaf emerges into the main stream and is washed further down the estuary. Soon the leaf comes to a sand bar. This impediment to the flow of the tide creates small waves in the water. But to the ant these seem like huge cataracts. Once over the bar the water becomes calm and another gust of wind arises and pushes the leaf with the hapless ant aboard to an overhanging branch. The ant quickly grasps the branch and hauls itself out of the water. It sits exhausted for a while on the branch, its little heart beating furiously. 'Whew,' it thinks to itself, 'I'll never go near the sea again. What a treacherous place it is, with whirlpools and cataracts and mountainous waves.'"

"The poor thing," exclaimed the Princess. "What a traumatic experience!"

Augustus resumed. "All the while the ant was enduring its journey down the estuary, a sea-eagle was soaring high overhead. The warm sun created a strong thermal that enabled it to hover effortlessly above the estuary. 'What a lovely day,' thinks the bird. 'The estuary is so calm and beautiful. I feel at one with the world.' What the ant saw as frightful and traumatic, the sea-eagle saw as tranquil and beautiful."

"We are like the green ant and the sea-eagle. Those self obsessed and driven by fear see the world as a frightening place. They are compelled, through no fault of their own, to be defensive and pessimistic."

"Why do you say, 'through no fault of their own'?"

"It is because our behaviour is greatly influenced by our genetics and our early learning experiences, both of which we have no control over. Princess, can you tell me a little about your childhood and your relationship with your mother".

Naomi lowered her eyes. A month or two ago she would have found this a most impertinent question. But now she trusted Augustus and knew implicitly that he was trying to help her.

"People tell me I was a good child. I know I tried very hard to please my mother. She told me that when I was good I made her happy. When she was happy she was lovely to be with and showered compliments and gifts on me. But then I came to believe that if being good made her happy, when she was sad I was perhaps also responsible for her unhappiness. So when she fell into the arms of despair I would redouble my efforts to do the things that would please her. You don't know the guilt I felt when she was sad and withdrawn."

Tears came to her eyes. Augustus nodded, encouraging her to keep talking.

"Years after she died, I started to believe that maybe I was even responsible for her death. That was so hard to contend with." The Princess wept openly.

"I suspected that you might have had such dysfunctional beliefs," said Augustus.

"Why do you say they are dysfunctional? Surely my behaviour contributed to my mother's distress?"

"Not at all," responded Augustus. "Your mother used this technique to manipulate you. Oh, and don't get me wrong, she didn't do it deliberately. It was something she, like you, through no fault of her own, unconsciously learned."

He continued, "You are not responsible for her or any one else's happiness. A person's psychological well-being is entirely their own responsibility. I could understand why there might be a connection to her suffering if you were doing physical things to your mother. If you hit her or bit her or kicked her, then that would surely cause her physical discomfiture. But your mother's mental state was not your responsibility. If you were messy, didn't do as you were told, or befriended people she didn't approve of, there was no causal connection between your behaviour and her internal sense of well-being. She was merely using her suffering to try and manipulate you to do things the way she wanted. This is not unusual. Many parents act this way. And they are not to blame, because they learn it from their parents and significant others around them."

"The unintended consequence was that you thought that somehow you were responsible for your mother's sense of well-being and that is indeed a heavy burden. Let me state it quite plainly for you—you can not directly influence a person's self-concept by your manifest behaviour. You are not responsible for how they feel about themselves. On the other hand, the important corollary that you must learn is that you, also, are responsible for your own internal sense of well-being."

"Why is it Augustus, that we continue to behave in these ways, even though, as you say, they are dysfunctional?"

"Well, Princess, like all animals our behaviours become habituated. If you go down to the bazaar, sometimes there will be an elephant. The elephant's owner knocks a peg into the ground and ties the animal to it. Although the animal has the strength to easily pull that peg out of the ground, it just obediently stays tethered to the peg. Why is this so? When the animal was small it was tethered to something substantial— perhaps a tree. It struggled to escape but to no avail. Eventually it gave up struggling because it had the perception that whatever it was tethered to was immovable. Once it had adopted this frame of mind, the owner could tether it to anything, however fragile, and it would not test its strength against it. In the same way human beings habituate their behaviour. Things that they did that might have got some positive reward, however long ago, are repeated over and over, even when they are no longer rewarded and are often grossly inappropriate. Similarly, those things that we tried, and were not effective at the time have been erased from our behavioural repertoire. Strategies that we learn to manipulate others, like suffering and anger, can just as easily become habituated as the elephant's docile acceptance of its tethering. And the erroneous learning associated with this is that if our behaviours seem to cause these effects on others then we must somehow be responsible for their emotional well-being."

The Princess seemed a little startled. "You are challenging a concept that has obviously been embedded in my thinking and has greatly shaped my life."

"Indeed I am. And this is something very important for your recovery. Accept responsibility for how you feel about yourself, but do not accept responsibility for how others feel about themselves. It is not 'love' to help another prop up facades that will inevitably bring them pain. 'Love' is often confronting and hard-edged if it is to be effective. 'Soft love' often merely reinforces wrong-minded behaviour that leads to prolonged suffering."

Naomi smiled. "Is that why you don't pander to me when I am sad, you heartless man?"

"My Lady, you have so many wonderful attributes, why should I encourage those that are not? But come let us now resume our practice. As we talked a while ago, I want you to observe your thoughts as they arise and then put them gently aside to still your mind. Then I want you to observe your emotions and, like the clouds, be detached from them and watch them pass. And remember, even your positive emotions will pass, just as you observe and wish for your negative emotions to pass."

They resumed their practice. When they had finished the Princess arose. "I am feeling better Augustus. You have no doubt helped me. But Augustus when can you take me to this special place where I can find peace? I yearn to be there and away from the suffering that my mind imposes on me. When I am ready will I have to go far?"

"When you are ready you will already know the way. When you are ready the place is so close you will be surprised." Augustus smiled enigmatically.

CHAPTER 17

> "In the attitude of silence the soul finds the path in a
> clearer light, and what is elusive and deceptive resolves
> itself into crystal clearness. Our life is a long and arduous
> quest after Truth."
>
> Mahatma Gandhi

Augustus sat with the Grand Vizier in an alcove in the palace garden.

"Tell me, Abdullah, you have known the Princess all her life—putting aside what you call her depression, what is she like? Can you describe her principal characteristics?"

"I will try." The Grand Vizier sat and mused a while. After a minute or two he responded, "My principal recollections of Naomi, without her affliction, are of a very generous, kind young lady. When not in the grip of her malaise she was always concerned for others. Perhaps sometimes she seemed to try too hard to want to please others."

He sighed, "I suspect that was certainly the case with her mother."

Abdullah resumed, "I am sure the respect she built among those around her, like her hand-maiden Asma, is why they have remained steadfast in their support during her illness."

"I am not surprised," said Augustus. "Those that become self-denigrating are often essentially good people that are appalled by their own apparent shortcomings. It is far easier for those that have little concern for the world about them to dismiss and disregard their perceived shortcomings. Naomi's condition stems from the fact that she cares for the world but has undue expectations about her own role in it. When she doesn't meet up with her own inflated ideals she retreats into the condition you call depression. As you have rightly indicated she has some feelings of guilt about her relationship with her mother and to some extent blames herself for her mother's suffering. It is surprising that such people have far higher expectations of themselves than they do of others. The foibles that they take so seriously would easily be forgiven if they were exemplified in someone close to them. Yet these same characteristics seem unforgiveable in themselves."

"You have eased the Princess's condition greatly, Augustus. The Sultan is very pleased. Can you tell me what is your methodology?"

"We have made some progress," Augustus conceded "But there is some more work to do to render the Princess more resilient."

"Nevertheless," responded Abdullah, "the princess is far happier now then before you came. What do you do? How does it work?"

Augustus smiled at the Grand Vizier. He had a great respect for Abdullah because he had seen how he conducted himself in the Sultan's court. He was a man of integrity and compassion. He had been quick to assist Augustus whenever he had asked for help. Augustus regularly met with him because of the Sultan's injunction on that first day that Augustus should report to him on his progress with the Princess. And Augustus had been moved by the way he had treated young Babak.

"You know, Abdullah, that almost every psychological problem that human beings confront, can be traced back to a person's self-concept. The problem with people with Naomi's condition is that not only do they have low self-esteem, but they have internal processes that are self-denigrating. As a result, once there is a problem they tend to spiral down in despair. They berate themselves for being incompetent and unable to cope. Most of us, with a more positive frame of mind, when encountering a difficulty will argue that it will soon pass, it will not dominate our lives and that often it hasn't resulted entirely from our personal failures but there have been other contributing factors. For people like Naomi, when they encounter a difficulty they will despair that it is a permanent issue impacting all areas of their lives and that they, personally, are responsible for the problem."[3]

---

[3] These concepts are developed in Martin Seligman's book, **Learned Optimism**.

The Grand Vizier nodded in understanding. "Those are vastly different outlooks that you describe."

"Indeed," said Augustus, "and in the process the people with the more pessimistic outlook, become self-obsessed in a morbid way. You know it has been rightfully said that well-adjusted people don't think less of themselves, they just think of themselves less."

"So what is it that you are doing that seeks to counter this process in the Princess?"

"Well I have been trying to work on strategies such that she might 'think of herself less!' To begin with I have taught her how to meditate."

"How does that work, my friend. When I see her there cross-legged on the floor, it seems to me that she has an even greater opportunity to indulge in self-criticism and be engulfed by her sadness."

Augustus chuckled. "That is because you do not understand the process of meditation. Meditation teaches us to cease the self-talk that our minds are continually engaging in. So rather than offering the Princess more opportunity for self-indulgence it offers an opportunity to escape from her self denigration. It offers a pause, indeed a recuperative space for the Princess."

"And is that all there is to it?"

"Oh no! That is merely the beginning. Meditation, properly practiced, makes people more self-aware. They become more attuned to their emotions and moods. They are able to disengage themselves from their emotions and moods and look more objectively at their real selves. There are other tools as well. To begin with I make sure the Princess has some positive affirmations every day to counter her self-criticisms. I have sought the cooperation of those she respects to give positive reinforcement when she is behaving in a more positive way. Previously she was being reinforced in her negative behaviour."

"I can see the value in all that. And I suspect that our indulgence of the Princess in the past was not helpful."

"That is true, but it is natural for us to want to console and cheer up those who are unhappy. It was because you all had showed such concern for the Princess that I knew I could enlist your help in assisting in my processes."

The two sat silently for a minute before Augustus continued. "The outcome I am seeking most for Naomi is to have her see the world differently. The Buddha taught that it is the nature of human beings in this imperfect world to suffer. We suffer because we become attached to things that are impermanent. Then we suffer from their loss or our anticipation of their loss. We construct huge psychic barriers to seek to retain what can not in the end be retained. Then in the Noble Eightfold Path, the Buddha taught us how to overcome suffering. The first step along the path is Right View. This simply means to see and understand things as they really are. Oft times we have been conditioned to see the world in an inappropriate way. The Princess learnt to believe that she was responsible for her mother's sense of well-being. Her mother by all accounts was often sad, which resulted in Naomi feeling responsible for her mother's gloomy moods."

Abdullah nodded his head. "The Princess's mother was of much the same disposition as the Princess. Many of us were concerned that the condition was hereditary and therefore beyond treatment."

"It seems to me," responded Augustus, "that our genetics do in some way dispose us to this sort of behaviour. But I must confess that what Naomi has **learnt** from her mother's example seems to me to be at least as great an influence on her behaviour."

"But what about her father?" Augustus continued. "No doubt some of his attributes will be shared by her also."

"The Sultan is a great leader—generous and compassionate. He is greatly loved by the people. Whereas Naomi's mother's temperament was often sombre and pessimistic, the Sultan is normally ebullient and optimistic. The only time I have seen him close to despair was when he was struggling to know how to help Naomi."

"Does he have any obvious character traits that are not helpful?" enquired Augustus.

"Augustus you should know better than to ask the Grand Vizier to criticise his sultan!" laughed Abdullah.

Augustus smiled. "But you know as well as I do Grand Vizier, that even sultans are not perfect—in fact I am sure there are some very imperfect sultans!"

"Well I know I can trust in your confidentiality and I suppose it might be helpful for you in your work if I tried to answer your question. I genuinely admire the Sultan and it is a great privilege to work for him. But if I were to single out something that might be labelled as a fault, I would say that the Sultan is not very worldly. I suppose that it comes from living such a cloistered life. You see, when people bring instances of suffering or need to his attention he normally does what he can do to help. But when you mix with princes and potentates and deal largely with courts and courtiers you come to believe that the suffering and the needy are a small minority. He would be surprised to know how many of his subjects could be so classified. Indeed barely a stone's throw from his palace gates there are many so afflicted. I know this because I do commerce there. But he is not aware of it and when I raise such issues he accuses me of demeaning him and the state of his suzerainty. It is a difficult issue for me."

Augustus nodded. "I am sure it is." But then he stopped because he could hear footsteps approaching and did not want to compromise Abdullah with further discussion of the Sultan's failings.

Before Augustus could continue, an official from the court appeared. "Effendi, the Sultan seeks your counsel."

Abdullah looked at Augustus. "It seems I must go Augustus. Can we continue this conversation another time? I am intrigued by your thinking and would like to learn more from you."

"Of course my friend—but don't be too modest, because I know there is much I can learn from you as well."

CHAPTER 18

"To perceive the world differently, we must be willing to
change our belief system, let the past slip away, expand our
sense of now, and dissolve the fear in our minds."

William James

One morning when Augustus was sitting in the ante-room waiting for
the Princess to arrive, the hand-maiden Asma suddenly appeared.

"What is it, Asma?" enquired Augustus concerned for the Princess's
welfare.

"Do not be alarmed sir, the Princess has sent me to warn you that
she will be a little late this morning. Her father asked her to breakfast
with him to discuss some family matters. She advises she will perhaps
be a half hour late."

"Thank you, Asma."

The girl turned to go. "But before you go, how is Naomi?"

Asma turned to Augustus. "She is quite well this morning and
in good spirits. Your work with her has truly been a miracle," she
enthused.

"Not at all," replied the little Buddhist, "It has been merely teaching
her some ways of improving her resilience and getting her to see the
world differently. For the next phase of my work I will need some
further assistance from you."

"I would be pleased to help in any way that I can. What do you
want of me?"

"I just need some information. How long have you known the Princess?"

"I've known her for a long time, sir—perhaps fifteen years. You see my father has, for many years, been an adviser to the Sultan and lives in the palace with my mother. We came here when I was but a little girl. The Princess and I used to play in the garden together just like ordinary little girls. There were few children at the palace and I suppose it was natural that we gravitated together. Even though my father had told me she was the Princess—that meant little to me. She was just another little girl who was delightful to play with. We had such good times together and we grew quite close. Then the Princess's mother died and, some time after, she became withdrawn and serious. A little later, because of our relationship the Sultan asked my father if I would be her attendant. I readily agreed, because I love the Princess and it saddened me to see her fall into despair."

"What would you say, Asma, are the Princess's defining characteristics, leaving aside her melancholy?"

"Oh, Augustus, she is such a kind and generous person! Sometimes I think this contributes to her depression because she is dissatisfied, wanting to do more for others. When I was little she was always wanting to give her toys to me. Even now, she will sometimes surprise me with an unexpected gift for me and my family. She is very empathetic and the hurts and concerns of others weigh heavily on her. As I said, I have often thought that this was a contributing factor to her depression. She is underneath it all a wonderful person—but however good she might be it doesn't seem enough for her. She denigrates herself for not living up to the very high standards she expects of herself."

Asma's response surprised Augustus, because she had never previously addressed him by name. It seemed to him that it was an acknowledgment of her growing trust and shared purpose in wanting to assist the Princess. "Thank you, Asma. You are of course right that the Princess's inherent caring nature has contributed to her melancholy. You are a very caring and perceptive person yourself. The Sultan chose well when finding an attendant for the Princess."

The girl lowered her eyes and blushed. "May Allah bless you Augustus—but I find it a privilege to work for her. I fervently hope that you can render her life happier." She then turned and walked off.

Later in the day, Augustus went for a walk in the city again. After walking for a half hour he found himself in a quarter where there was great poverty. The children roamed the streets barely clothed and looking emaciated. Adults sat on the ground and hopelessness dulled their eyes. The housing was basic and inadequate to meet the needs of the burgeoning population. Beggars abounded. The streets were full of debris and human detritus. Augustus shuddered. This was a forlorn and desperate place. And it was barely more than a stone's throw from the Sultan's magnificent palace.

The little Buddhist frowned. The despair surrounding him contrasted dramatically with the sumptuous luxury of the palace.

He sat down on a low wall at the edge of a precinct dominated by a group of hovels. Their inhabitants were obviously very poor and would be struggling to survive.

All at once came a cheery shout.

"Augustus, Augustus! Mother, it is Augustus!"

And there emerging from one of the desolate huts came Babak. He ran from his humble dwelling and embraced the little Buddhist.

Augustus was surprised but pleased to see his little friend. "Well, young man—how fare you?"

"Oh Augustus, I am well and I am happy. My mother and my sisters are now well-fed and I am doing useful work in the palace gardens."

As he spoke a woman came striding purposefully towards them. Babak turned and excitedly cried, "Mother, mother—here he is. This is Augustus the benefactor I told you about."

The woman came and knelt before Augustus and taking his hand exclaimed. "Oh sir, I must express my gratitude for what you have done for us."

Augustus was uncomfortable with the obvious adulation.

"Oh no, my good woman, I have done very little."

"That is not what my son says."

"Then your son is prone to exaggerate. But it would help me to know a little about what it is like to live in poverty as so many seem to in this place."

She thought a moment and was about to speak but Babak interjected.

"Forgive me mother, but I owe this to my benefactor. First of all Augustus there is starvation. Most of our neighbours, as was the case for us, do not have enough to eat. It is heart-wrenching for parents to see their children starve. It is cruel to see your siblings without enough to eat. I myself was driven to theft by that imperative. I would rather have died at the whim of the Sultan's guards than see my mother and my sisters suffer so."

Augustus nodded and whilst he sought to be stoic he could not prevent a tear from sliding down his face.

But now the boy's mother interjected, "But you know Augustus, as much as starvation impacts the body, meaninglessness impacts the soul. Not having something useful to do resigns us to hopelessness. Most of those in this place suffer from this affliction. My son has been working for the Sultan for a month or two now and merely having something useful to contribute seems to make a great deal of difference to him. Being gainfully employed is as satisfying as not being hungry. His meeting you has turned his life around. You have also shown him the folly of pursuing materialistic outcomes. As your friend Abdullah pointed out, you do not seem to be wealthy but you seem to be happy. You seem, in fact to have very little and yet you were prepared to share with him what little you had. I will never forget your generosity."

She paused a while before continuing.

"I do not know what you did with my son, sir, but I thank you for it. Certainly we have benefitted materally from the money your friend gave him, and from the money he earns working for the Sultan, but his greatest gift is his compassion and tolerance. He always had such tendencies but his meeting with you has increased these attributes."

Babak held his mother tightly and then said to Augustus, "Would you like to meet my sisters?"

Augustus quickly responded, "I would be delighted to meet your sisters!"

The boy and his mother led Augustus back to their humble abode. They passed in through the doorway and there sitting on the tamped earth floor were two little girls. They were beautiful little girls. Augustus was moved. He thought about Babak's motives. He was never trying to steal for his own personal benefit. He could see from the admiration in his eyes that his efforts were directed to the welfare of his mother and his two little sisters.

They sat together on a plain mat on the dirt floor and chatted for a while. Finally Augustus bade his farewells, and with the blessings of the little family ringing in his ears made his way back to the palace.

He found the poverty very disquieting. His natural empathy for the poor made it a difficult journey for him. But then he remembered the Princess's ambition to help the disadvantaged. Perhaps there might be a way of engaging the Princess's concern to improve the welfare of these unfortunates. Despite the squalor of the streets, a wry smile came to his face and he walked back to the palace deep in thought.

CHAPTER 19

"If we could see the miracle of a single flower clearly, our
whole life would change."

Buddha

The weeks passed and Augustus continued his work with the Princess.
She was now largely of good cheer and came happily to him each
morning and evening. They would meditate together and Augustus
could see that her meditation practice was helping her still her troubled
mind and she now seemed easily to be able to cease her mind chatter.
But there were odd occasions when she seemed overwhelmed by despair.
These incidents however were less frequent and the Princess seemed to
understand that they were temporary aberrations and that she now had
tools to help her overcome her emotional distress.

One morning as they walked together, with Asma in attendance, in
the palace garden, Augustus pointed out a beautiful flower to her. She
looked briefly at it, nodded her approval and was about to walk on.

"No, no," counseled Augustus, "Savour its beauty."

She turned to look again.

Augustus said slowly and deliberately, "Look at its lustrous colour.
See how the red fades to pink at the edge of the petals. Look at the
scalloped edges of the petals. Notice the yellow stamens. Smell the sweet
scent. Look at the contrast between the petals and the deep green of
the leaves."

The Princess stood motionless for minutes. Finally she looked up.
"Oh, Augustus—that was beautiful. I don't think I've ever really seen

a flower properly before. I have noticed them—but never really seen one in the way you have shown me."

"It is a good lesson, Princess. Human beings seem so disposed to dwell on what is ugly, painful or sorrowful. It is useful that we should counter this by dwelling on what is beautiful, uplifting and pleasant. Savour these moments and relive them. Sit now with me on this bench. Be still a moment and tell me what you hear."

They sat together on a wooden bench. The hand-maiden, Asma, sat on a low rock wall a little way off and watched with interest this interaction with her mistress.

After a little while, the Princess turned to the little Buddhist. "I can hear the sweet song of a bird."

Augustus nodded but said nothing.

The Princess sat a while longer. A minute or two passed. "I can hear the rustling in the wind of the leaves of this tree."

Again Augustus nodded and then he said, "Meditate awhile and still your thoughts and then tell me what you hear."

Naomi went into her meditation practice. Perhaps five minutes passed. Augustus interrupted. "That is enough. What did you hear?"

The princess smiled. "I heard a cicada's drone. I could hear the rumbling of cart wheels on cobblestones somewhere in the distance. There was the sound of a bee buzzing. And when I listened intently what I had thought was a bird's song was indeed two different birds calling. There was also the sound of a tree limb gently rubbing on another."

Augustus beamed. "Very good," he said. "You see how meditation improves your awareness. There are two benefits of this. Firstly, you are more in touch with your environment. But secondly, it helps you get in touch with your own emotional state. When you are so receptive to sensory inputs it is far easier to objectively monitor your own emotions. Rather than identify with them, in this state you will be able to dispassionately observe how you are responding to the world. This gives you the latitude to intervene in a helpful way. In my tradition we call this mindfulness. When we still the inner chatter of our minds we are far more in the present and able to appreciate the world."

"Well, I am not sure I can do that yet, Augustus, but I can see how my awareness of my physical environment has been improved."

Augustus nodded. "You know," he said, "When I lived with my Master, Takygulpa Rinpoche, a sage came to visit us. When he arrived the Master was away attending to an issue in another village. He had heard of my Master's wisdom and wanted to know some details of his practice. He asked me, 'What does your Master pay most attention to?' I laughed and responded, 'Whatever he is doing at the time.' He shook his head in disbelief. But this is in essence the practice of mindfulness. We engage ourselves fully in what is happening *now* with no concern of the past or the future. We need to engage as fully as possible, with all our senses, in the present moment."

They sat silently together for a while and then Augustus asked, "My Lady, it would be helpful for me to know about your aspirations. What is it that you would do that would bring you gratification in the long term?"

The princess contemplated for a long time. Augustus waited patiently, as ever, and then finally the Princess replied, "There are perhaps two things that would cause me joy. Firstly, I want to please my father. He has been so loving to me that it would be gratifying to know that he was aware how much I appreciate that love."

Augustus nodded sympathetically. "There is no doubt in my mind, Princess, that that is already the case. It is not the time now to go into it, and you are not yet in a frame of mind to agree, but I must tell you that you do not need your father's love to be happy. You just need to be able to accept yourself and your part in the world. Serenity comes from your state of mind. Not that you should not appreciate your father's love. It is of great comfort to you now and is part of the support platform that is aiding your recovery. Real love, of course, is that love that is given with no expectation of anything in return. It is unconditional love—love without conditions, given as a gift."

"That is true, Augustus. I understand that and there is nothing that could happen that would change my love for my father. And when I think of the years he has loved me without my giving him anything in return, there can be no doubt of his unconditional love. I just want him to know how special that is to me."

"After that," she continued, "I would be pleased if I could make a contribution to the less fortunate of the world. I am in a very privileged place, being the daughter of the Sultan. I often feel unworthy of this exalted position. My heart would be lighter if I could use my good fortune to benefit the poor, the disadvantaged and those that are cut off from the world."

"That is a good thing to do. You see compassion not only helps others—it is also beneficial to you. The practice of compassion is like a meditation that restores serenity when you are agitated. It is a great tranquiliser! You might remember our previous discussions about how people in your condition become self-obsessed. Compassion is the antidote to this. Buddhist scriptures tell of the bodhisattvas, who reach a high level of spiritual attainment through practices focused on compassion. They can attain great happiness and well-being by developing extraordinary degrees of compassion and loving kindness."

"I don't think I have the dedication to be a bodhisattva," replied the Princess, "but I would like to make a worthwhile contribution to the needy of our community."

"Then perhaps you will allow me to find a way for you to indulge that ambition," said Augustus.

"How so?" enquired the Princess, genuinely intrigued.

"We will see tomorrow," replied Augustus. "Come prepared to go out into the city."

The Princess frowned. "I can't do that without my father's permission and he will never let me outside the palace without a bodyguard."

"Well, my Princess, go to your father and make this request and if he is agreeable tomorrow we will sojourn out into the city."

"So be it," responded the Princess.

"You know Augustus, that when you enquire of my aspirations, my greatest aspiration is to go to that special place that you have described to me, where I will be happy. I am cognisant of the fact that my life is much more bearable than it was, thanks to you—but I really yearn to enter that special place you have told me about. What is it like? Are there trees? Are there birds? Are there streams?"

Augustus smiled. "It is not a physical place you already know. It is a state of mind. It is something already close to you. But when the time comes you will see it differently. When you change at the deepest level, as you are beginning to do so, your worldview changes. A sage once said, 'We don't see things as **they** are. We see things as **we** are.'

Therefore it often helps us to see the world as a more benign place when our state of mind changes."

"That is all very puzzling to me, Augustus. But I am anxious to be there. When can you take me there?"

"Soon, my Princess, you will be ready. I suspect that it will surprise you that you have not found it before."

CHAPTER 20

"If you want others to be happy, practice compassion.
If you want to be happy, practice compassion."

The Dalai Lama

On the next morning the Princess came to Augustus. They went through their usual routine. Naomi told Augustus that her father was well, and that Asma was well also.

She was pleased that her father had given her a necklace. She showed it to Augustus. "Look Augustus at this beautiful thing my father has given me. Do you know what he said?"

"Well, no My Lady—I have no idea about what he said."

"He said to me, 'My daughter, I have so enjoyed your company in these last few months that I wanted to express my appreciation. I have come to enjoy my time with you more than anything I do. Once, when you were depressed it was difficult to engage with you and it saddened me greatly that I could not converse with you. Your company is now so enjoyable that I treasure every minute I have with you.'"

Augustus smiled. "The necklace is indeed beautiful, but I suspect your father's words were more important to you."

Naomi looked up at him and smiled. "Of course. There is nothing my father could give me that pleased me more than his approval. I will value this necklace, not for its material value but for how it reflects my father's love for me. He has been so patient with me and supported me through my darkest times. Unfortunately, I am not able to see him again for some time."

Naomi looked a little sad.

"Why will you not be able to meet with your father?" enquired Augustus.

"He has a long journey to take to attend to some affairs of state. I will pray for his safety and speedy return."

"I should caution you also to take care that you don't become too attached to your father's approval. You can be happy without it. I am sure you enjoy seeing your father pleased and because you love him you can join in his pleasure. But be careful of falling into the same trap as you did with your mother."

"What do you mean?"

"You became dependant on your mother's approval and convinced that you were somehow responsible for her sense of well-being. Now we have seen that you couldn't be held responsible for your mother's condition. Partly it was due to genetic factors and partly to learned behaviours. She would have learned many of those behaviours long before you came along. It is good that you do things that please your father. But remember to do so with the right motives. Don't do it for his approval—do it because you love him."

Naomi sat deep in thought mulling over Augustus's words. Before she could respond she heard the little Buddhist chuckle.

"Why do you laugh?" she asked in surprise.

"I was just remembering a story my Master told me once about some other princesses. Would you like to hear it?"

Naomi enjoyed Augustus's little stories. "Yes please," she responded.

"In the time of Chan Huang there lived in an outer province a powerful emperor. The emperor had married a famous beauty and over the years they had four daughters. The empress was devoted to her four princesses. The princesses dearly loved their mother and vied for her attention. One morning, after their daily instruction, the empress led them to the palace gardens.

'Play here a while,' she said. 'I have some household matters to attend to. I will return as soon as I am able.'

The gardens were huge and immaculately kept. The empress loved flowers and so the garden was replete with flower beds. The girls played together for a while and then the oldest one went off by herself. In time, missing their sister, the next two older girls went off to find her, leaving the youngest to play by herself. Sisters two and three came upon the oldest girl sitting on a grassy bank with a huge bunch of flowers near her. She was putting them in her hair and into the folds of her clothes. As well she held the prettiest flowers of all in her lap.

'What are you doing?' they asked the oldest princess.

'I am making myself pretty for Mama. Surely if I am the prettiest she will then love me most of all.' Spurred on by this threat the other two girls rushed off to match their sister. They covered themselves with flowers so that they might also compete for their mother's affection.

Soon they were arguing about who was most beautiful. They fought over the flowers they thought might best enhance their appearances and unfortunately destroyed many in the process. Then they looked up and could see their mother approaching in the distance. So they hurriedly covered themselves in blooms and awaited their mother's return.

In a few short minutes the empress had walked to within a few metres of the older girls. The empress was not only beautiful but she was also wise. As she approached, she cast her eyes over the flower bedecked girls in front of her and mused out loud, 'Where have my beautiful princesses gone?'

Before the older girls could say a thing, she continued, 'Oh there is one of them.' Nearby, running helter-skelter towards her, came the youngest princess. She held a single white flower in her hand.

The empress and the youngest sister embraced fondly. 'What have you there my dear,' asked the empress looking at the beautiful white bloom clutched in the eager little hand. 'Have you found a flower to help make you beautiful?'

The little girl frowned. 'No, mother. I have no need for that. I have brought a flower as a gift for you. It smelt so beautiful I wanted you to have it.'

'Why thank you my dear. You do indeed have a beauty that no flower could enhance.' The empress kissed the little girl and hand in hand they walked away down the garden path.

The older girls looked at each other disconsolately. Then all of a sudden, a great wind sprang up. It pulled the flowers from their hair and their clothes and scattered them over the grass. 'Stupid flowers,' said the oldest as the blooms were strewn far and wide.

'It is not the flowers that are stupid!' exclaimed another. 'We are. We never needed flowers to make our mother love us. And would we want her to love us for being beautiful or smart or nimble or dexterous? They are largely things we have no choice over. Wouldn't it be better if she just loved us for who we are? What's more, if that is the case, we have no need to compete for her affections. We can then love each other for who we are as well.' The other two nodded their acceptance of this wisdom.

'I'll go and get a basket,' said one. 'Then we can gather all the flowers up for mother'. And so they did. The wind had stopped and they enjoyed themselves gathering up the flowers and putting them in the basket. They laughed and skipped and played. They were enjoying themselves so much that they did not see their mother approaching again with the youngest princess. When she was close, she called out joyfully, 'Why, here are my beautiful princesses. It is so nice to see them again.' Then they all ran to her and embraced."

The Princess clapped her hands. "Why that was lovely, Augustus— and so wise."

Augustus smiled. "Let us now begin our practice."

They sat on the ground and began their meditation. After a time, Augustus arose and said, "That will be enough for now. Now tell me, has your father given you permission to venture out into the city?"

Naomi nodded. "But as I conveyed to you, I must be accompanied by my bodyguard."

"Then go and fetch your bodyguard and I will meet you at the palace gates in half an hour."

CHAPTER 21

"We think sometimes that poverty is only being hungry,
naked and homeless. The poverty of being unwanted,
unloved and uncared for is the greatest poverty."
Mother Teresa of Calcutta

At the due time, Naomi arrived at the palace gates. Augustus could tell she was excited. Having spent most of her life confined by the palace walls, this represented a significant adventure for the young princess. He remembered his discussion with Abdullah about the Sultan's lack of worldliness. He feared this would apply even more so to the princess and that the poverty and the squalor she was about to see might prove somewhat traumatic to her. But he was convinced this must be done so that he might be able to try and set up a platform for her to exercise the empathy and generosity which both Asma and Abdullah had assured him were some of her strengths.

The bodyguard was a large muscular young man in traditional garb. There was a broad belt around his waist. A scabbard hung from it sheathing a very imposing scimitar.

"This is Hasim," said Naomi introducing the young man. "My father has decreed he must travel with me outside the palace walls."

Augustus smiled and bowed courteously towards the bodyguard. "Greetings, Hasim. I am Augustus."

Hasim nodded his acknowledgement and the three set off into the city.

The Princess was interested and stimulated by the sights she saw in the city. She had seldom been beyond the palace walls except to ride in the countryside with her father. But they were able to make their way into the rural landscape by going to the East, away from the city.

Today they walked to the West. Naomi was intrigued by the commerce that she witnessed—people coming and going, haggling and trading and promoting their wares. She was most interested in the bazaar with its colourful stalls and exotic goods and produce. They stopped for a while and watched the street performers entertain the crowd. These people were so different from those she encountered in her father's court.

Then as Augustus led them further, the alleyways became narrow and dim. Now, many they passed were obviously poor, perhaps destitute. Some begged for alms and Augustus would give them a coin or two from the little leather bag attached to the sash of his robe. The Princess frowned. She was obviously upset by the sight of the poor. Her cloistered life had kept her sheltered from the realisation that a mere half hour's walk from the palace there were such people.

As they walked, they could see that not only were these peasants poor but there were many among them that were crippled or suffering illness and disease. After a time, noticing the growing distress of his mistress Hasim said, "Perhaps Princess it might be better if we went back."

Naomi shook her head. "No, Hasim I want to see for myself the suffering of our people. I had not realised that such poverty and distress existed almost in our own back yard."

On the very outskirts of the city, they came upon a place where there was only makeshift housing and the streets were full of litter. The smell was nauseating. There were tears in the princess's eyes now. "Oh Augustus," she murmured, "How can people live like this?"

"They largely have no alternative, my lady. Nobody chooses to live this way."

A half dozen children milled around them clambering for attention. They begged for money and food. Augustus turned his leather pouch inside out but there were now only a few coins left. He patted their heads and gave them the remainder of his money and they rushed off excitedly to their homes. The impoverishment, the suffering and the despair was obvious and disturbing.

Behind the last row of the dishevelled, meagre dwellings was a small olive grove. Naomi noticed that there was a woman sitting under the largest tree cradling a child in her arms. The Princess walked over to the olive grove. The woman looked up at her despairingly.

Naomi sat down beside her. "You seem distraught," she said. "What is concerning you?"

The woman just shook her head.

Naomi persisted, "What is the matter?"

The woman sat silently awhile. Then she turned and looked at the Princess. "You seem someone of privileged rank. I do not think you could possibly understand my circumstances."

Naomi hung her head. "I am sorry you feel that way, but I would really like to understand what causes your distress."

The woman sighed. "I am called Basheera. I am distressed because my husband recently died leaving me alone with my daughter. He was such a loving man and I was blessed to be his wife. But he had gone to work in the provinces, far from our families and I, of course, went with him. When he died I tried to find some of our kin. I had a sister who lived here and I walked many days to return here to try and find her, but when I arrived I am told she has gone. Now I have nothing, no one to turn to and nowhere to go. And I have my little one to care for. What am I to do?"

The Princess was overcome with pity for the distressed woman. She looked at Augustus. "I have no more to give, my lady", he said looking at his empty pouch.

The Princess shook her head in dismay. Augustus could see that she was dealing with a substantial internal struggle. Finally, she said, "Take this," and she lifted from her neck the precious necklace her father had given her. "I am sure you will be able to trade this for something substantial."

Augustus opened his eyes wide in wonder. This was an extraordinarily generous thing to do. He turned to the woman and said, "Be careful that you get the full worth of this gift that the Princess has given you because it is a very valuable necklace."

"Princess?" queried Basheera. "Who is this that has shown such benevolence towards me?"

"This," said Augustus "is the Princess Naomi, the daughter of the Sultan. She has a concern for the poor and the unfortunate in the suzerainty."

"That is plain to see. I thank you my lady for your exceeding generosity."

So saying the woman took Naomi's hand and kissed it."

Naomi was nonplussed. She placed her hand consolingly upon the woman's shoulder. "There is no need to thank me. I would be gratified if you could secure food and lodging for yourself and your child."

Augustus again interjected. "As you can see the Princess is concerned for you. We will come again tomorrow in the late afternoon. If you can, please be here, so that we might check on your welfare."

"You have been very generous," said the woman. "I will exchange your jewellery for what I can get in the bazaar and I will try to be here to see you again at this time tomorrow."

CHAPTER 22

"Happiness often sneaks in through a door you didn't
know you'd left open."

John Barrymore

Basheera's heart beat quickly. She stood and watched the three figures merge into the crowd in the distance. She stood holding the hand of her child in one hand and clutching the necklace in the other.

She was perplexed. How could she trade the necklace—convert its value into money to pay for her shelter and her food? Eventually, plucking up her courage she ventured into the bazaar. She came to a stall where a man was selling jewellery. She waited until his customers had been dealt with and the man stood alone in front of his wares. This was difficult for her but she knew she must try to sell the necklace.

Approaching him she asked, "Do you buy jewellery, sir?"

The man looked suspiciously at Basheera. He nodded. "Sometimes," he said. "Why do you ask?"

"I have a valuable piece I would dispose of." Still clutching the necklace tightly she put it in front of him. He went to take it off her. "No, do not touch it," she said. "Just tell me what you think it is worth."

"Madam, I can't value the piece without properly examining it."

"Just give me an estimate of its worth."

"How did you come by it? It is unusual for someone of your station in life to have such jewellery."

"I can not tell you," she replied frostily.

"I suspect you must have stolen it."

"I did not!" she indignantly replied.

The trader shrugged his shoulders in resignation. He then offered her a paltry amount saying it was obvious that the necklace was tainted. Tears came to Basheera's eyes. "You seek to take advantage of me," said Basheera. She turned on her heel and walked off with her child.

The trader laughed. "When you find you can't sell it, you'll be back," he taunted.

Indeed Basheera tried her luck with three more dealers and none would make a reasonable offer. They each seemed to sense her urgent need and tried to acquire the necklace at greatly devalued prices. And as before they were suspicious of how she might have come to have such a prized possession. She was discouraged now. She sat on a stool at the edge of the bazaar nursing her daughter and wept.

Finally, she stood up. "This is no good," she said to herself, "sitting here weeping will not provide for me and my child. I will try again."

To her left in a corner away from the bazaar proper stood a little stall. There was little on display here but what was there, was of the most exquisite quality. The trader was talking to a distinguished looking well-dressed man. Basheera stood patiently a metre or two back waiting for them to end their conversation.

After a time the well-dressed man became aware of her presence. He addressed the trader and said, "Jawad, it seems you have a client. I will wait while you tend to her." Then he turned and looked at Basheera. His concern was immediately aroused when he viewed the woman and her child.

Somewhat reluctantly, Jawad turned to Basheera and said, "What can I do for you, Madam?"

"Sir I have jewellery that I would sell. Can you tell me what you might offer for this piece?"

Jawad looked up and down at her and sniffed in a dismissive way. "Someone such as you can not have jewellery of such significance, unless you stole it. I will not buy tainted goods."

Basheera was crestfallen. Again she had tried to sell the necklace, but to no avail. She went to walk away. However the well-dressed man intervened. "Don't go, Madam. I am familiar with the piece that you hold. It is of great value and I would purchase it from you if I can."

"Let me deal with this, Jawad," he said. He placed his arm on the woman's shoulder and led her a little away from the booth.

"This is the Princess's necklace," he stated. "How did you come by it?"

She was surprised that he had rightly identified the necklace. This man had a presence, a certain impressiveness that appealed to her. Basheera had been reluctant to tell any of the other traders her personal details, but this man, she felt, she could trust.

"My Lord, I met the Princess in the olive grove beyond the bazaar. I had my child with me and I told her of my misfortune. She was so sympathetic but she had nothing to give. Then in a gesture of supreme generosity she asked me to take the necklace and to sell it to care for myself and my child."

Basheera broke into tears. "There is no one in my whole life who has been so generous."

The well-dressed man put his arm gently on her shoulder and said, "Do not weep. You have been truly blessed. Tell me more about yourself."

Basheera told him her sad story—about how she had lost her husband and had come to Yolanpur only to find that there was nobody she could turn to.

Finally, the man said, "I will buy the necklace from you."

He took a little leather pouch from his robe and poured out an assortment of gold pieces.

"Here," he said, "This is what I shall pay you for the necklace."

Basheera was overwhelmed.

"But sir, that is far more than what the traders have offered."

"That is because they are charlatans and keen to take advantage of you. I know the true value of the piece because I am the one that purchased it for the Sultan to give to his daughter. I have some knowledge of these things, having friends who manufacture such trinkets. I am happy to pay you its full worth."

Basheera gave him the necklace. The man, in return gave her a handful of gold pieces, the like of which she had never seen in her life before.

"Oh sir," she exclaimed humbly, "You are the saviour of myself and my child"

The man smiled. "No, your primary beneficiary is the Princess, Naomi."

"Now come," he said. "We have to find you food and shelter. We cannot leave you and your child to fend for yourself in this vile place. Follow me."

He led the way through the maze of alleyways and streets. They walked for maybe ten minutes until they came to a stall where a goldsmith was working.

Basheera's companion hailed the goldsmith. "Ishmael, old friend, may I speak with you?"

The goldsmith was a slight old man with fair hair. He had a speckled beard and a twinkle in his eye. He was dressed in a white robe, and wore sandals upon his feet. He was bare headed. His fair hair, white robes and noble demeanour impressed Basheera and she felt comfortable in his presence. And just like her benefactor who had led her here, intuitively, she felt could trust him.

Basheera could tell just by looking at his slender hands that he was a skilled artisan. He was working on the gold filigree adorning a beautiful gemstone. He looked slowly up from his work and smiled at the man who had interrupted him. The warmth of the smile betrayed his affection for the newcomer. "But of course," came the reply. He pointed to some stools alongside his work bench. "Come and sit and make your friend comfortable as well."

"Ishmael, this is Basheera. She is a pilgrim in need of help. Can you provide for her for a little while until she can contact some of her family? I would trust you and your good wife to care for her. She has money to pay you for her accommodation and food."

Basheera nodded humbly at the old man and sat on the stool with her daughter on her lap.

The goldsmith ruffled the hair of the child. "This is a beautiful child that you have and it would not do to have either of you without somewhere to stay in this rough place. Of course we can provide for them," he said looking again at the well-dressed man.

The man in turn turned to Basheera. "My friend here has a number of enterprises. Not only does he manufacture magnificent pieces from gold, but he and his wife also run an inn where travellers can stay."

"We would be delighted to care for you," said Ishmael. "I do not want to pry, but could you tell me a little more about yourself."

With a little coaxing from her companion, Basheera told Ishmael her sorry story. She told of the death of her husband, her travails in coming to Yolanpur, and her good fortune in being gifted the necklace by the Princess. The goldsmith was intrigued. He sat awhile and caressed his sparse beard. Finally he said, "I may be able to help you further." He volunteered, "In pursuing my trade, I travel frequently. The township where your relative went is one that I visit occasionally. If you will but stay with us a while, I will be happy to take you there on my next trip."

Basheera was overjoyed. "You are both so good to me. Not only do I now have somewhere to stay and the wherewithal to sustain my daughter and myself, I now have the opportunity to rejoin my family. How my circumstances have changed in these last few hours!"

The goldsmith smiled. "We are more than happy to provide for you and your beautiful child."

The well-dressed man said, "Basheera, we owe Ishmael some rent. Show me the gold pieces I gave you." The woman took out the money. He withdrew from her hand a few gold pieces and gave them to Ishmael. "It would seem to me, friend, that this is enough for sustenance for Basheera and her child for a month or so and a little more. With the little extra perhaps you could persuade your good wife to take this poor lady and her child into the bazaar and help them buy some clothes so they might feel adequately attired."

Ishmael looked at the cluster of coins. "That is more than enough," he said. "Take the lady and her child now to the inn and acquaint them with my wife. They shall be properly cared for, I assure you. Give her the money and I am sure when it is convenient she will take our guest to the bazaar."

"I could ask for no more. Thank you, Ishmael, for your kindness."

Basheera knelt before him and exclaimed, "I am so grateful sir. You have given me hope in the midst of my despair."

The goldsmith shook his head. "Do not waste your gratitude on me. Remember the Princess who was so generous and this gentleman who is so caring. Their contributions to your welfare are greater than mine."

Nevertheless she hugged the old man and then carrying her daughter followed her other benefactor off to the inn.

The inn was a few minutes walk away. When they arrived at the inn the well-dressed man called out, "Lateefah, Lateefah, are you there?"

The inn was a sturdy building of timber and mud bricks. It was of two storeys with white-washed walls. After a moment there was movement upstairs and bye and bye an elderly lady made her way down the stairs and quietly asked, "Who is it that seeks after me?"

Basheer's companion responded, "It is only me, your old friend."

"Huh, you old villain," she called more boisterously now having recognized the visitor at the bottom of the stairs. "What are you doing here?"

She was tall and slender but a little stooped. Her face was wrinkled but the creases on her face seemed to reflect a life well-spent rather than just the outcome of age. She emanated a serenity that reflected a soul at ease with itself.

"I have come from Ishmael with a pilgrim that your worthy husband has agreed to take in."

Lateefah smiled. "That is just like him, the old goat. He takes in strangers and stray cats and has no thought of how I, the mistress of the household, will accommodate and care for them."

The words came in mock anger, but anyone could see in her eyes her concern for the newly arrived guests. "So who has the old reprobate foisted on me now?"

She turned and looked closely at Basheera and her daughter. Basheera had misread the old lady's playfulness and there was a little alarm in her voice. The poor woman cried out, "Oh please forgive us. We did not mean to impose on you in this way."

Her companion just laughed. "Do not concern yourself, Basheera. This lady pretends to be affronted but underneath she is full of compassion."

Even as he spoke Lateefah put her arm around the shoulder of Basheera's daughter and winked at her. "Oh I feel great sympathy for you, my child, if you had to place yourself at the mercy of this old imposter."

She looked at the well-dressed man and laughed.

"Well, come on you old ram. Introduce me to your travelling companions."

"This is Basheera and her daughter. Basheera's husband has recently died and she fled to Yolanpur believing there was a close relative here.

But unfortunately the relative has moved on. She and her child need somewhere to stay. They have money enough to provide for their sustenance and your worthy husband asked that I should bring them here to you."

The mirth which had lit up Lateefah's face was now clouded with compassion. She embraced the other woman and said, "May the Prophet have mercy on you."

Basheera looked gratefully at her and her male companion. "I think He already has shown His mercy."

The man nodded. He took the gold pieces from his pocket and handed them to Lateefah.

"This is the rent we agreed upon for you to care for these unfortunates for a month or so."

The old woman's eyes opened wide in surprise.

"This is a large payment for what you are asking of us. Are you sure Ishmael is not trying to rob you?" she asked with a smile.

"No, not at all," said the man. "This was the agreed amount."

Lateefah turned to Basheer.

She nodded and said, "This is what was agreed and I'm happy to pay it."

"Basheer has more money to provide further rent if her stay should be prolonged. But there is another favour I will ask of you," said the man.

"Would you mind waiting until I've looked after my guests?" she implored.

"Not at all," said the man.

"Come," said Lateefah turning to Basheer, "let me show you a room for you and your child."

She led them upstairs and opened a door into a large room with a bed and other basic furniture.

"Will this suit?" the old woman asked.

Basheera nodded enthusiastically. "This is excellent. I thank you so much."

Lateefah responded, "You are welcome to be part of our humble household. Make yourself comfortable. If you need anything I will be downstairs."

She returned downstairs. The well-dressed man sat at a table with her and chatted amiably for a while. After a time, the man arose and made his farewells. But before he went he turned to Lateefah and said, "Oh and by the way, I must explain the other favour I mentioned. Ishmael asked could you accompany Basheer out into the bazaar and help her purchase some clothes. As you can see, she seems to have brought nothing with her. That's why we added a little more into your rent. She has traded some jewellery with me, so if this is not enough let me know and I will supplement her monetary contribution to you."

Lateefah nodded. "I will be glad to do so and the money you have given me will easily pay her rent and buy clothes for them both."

The man smiled. "You are indeed an angel," he said he kissed her gently on her cheek and then walked off.

Later in the day Lateefah accompanied Basheera into the bazaar. They had an immediate attachment and Basheera was more than comfortable allowing Lateefah to assist her in purchasing a few necessities for her and her child. She nursed the child while Basheera examined the clothes on offer. The child bonded easily with the gentle old woman.

They returned to the inn with their purchases. Basheera laid them out on a table and they celebrated the shrewdness of their bartering skills and admired the quality of what they had acquired. They dressed the child in some of the new garments and commented on how lovely she looked. Lateefah made coffee and they talked and cemented a growing friendship.

CHAPTER 23

"What man actually needs is not a tensionless state but
rather the striving and struggling for some goal worthy
of him. What he needs is not the discharge of tension at
any cost, but the call of a potential meaning waiting to be
fulfilled by him."

Victor Frankl

After leaving Basheera clutching the beautiful necklace, the Princess, the Buddhist and the bodyguard all trudged back to the palace. Naomi did not talk at first because the plight of the poor had impacted so strongly upon her. Augustus could see she was immersed in her thinking and reliving the experience. Finally, Naomi turned to Augustus and said, "Oh Augustus, what are we going to do?"

Augustus smiled reassuringly at the Princess. "My Lady, we will do what we can do and be satisfied."

"What do you mean?"

"Someone in your state of mind often strives for perfection, the ideal, to right the wrongs of the world. But in the end we can only do what we can do. We will try to ease some of the suffering, and we will try to ease the pain but you must be resigned to the fact we can not right all the wrongs of the world."

"Oh, Augustus you sound so defeatist."

"Perhaps Princess—but I have learned that if I wait to take action until I have the perfect solution, nothing gets done. Let us do what we can and be satisfied. Can I speak frankly with you?"

"Of course. You have done so much to help me and I have come to know you are always genuinely trying to help me. I am wise enough now to know that I should listen to you."

"Thank you My Lady. Well, what I was about to say is that often people in your condition are locked into inactivity because they can not create a perfect outcome. A perfect outcome might be that all those in the city who are poor are nurtured and cared for. That is a marvelous ideal, but largely unattainable. The Buddha taught us that there will always be suffering no matter how hard we try to avoid it. It is our duty to do what we can and then be satisfied. Often a lot of good things are prevented because a perfect solution can't be found. I myself, am dedicated to reducing the impact of suffering in the world. However, I know that suffering is so pervasive in this world I can't eradicate it. I must do the best I can and be satisfied with that."

"I think I will be sad if even one of those poor people go hungry."

"It is alright to be sad, but if that sadness is manifested in the affliction that you call depression you will automatically negate any opportunity to help the poor. If you retire to your room and weep and become debilitated because of your sadness, many more will starve. If you are not captured by your demons we can at least help some of them. Whilst we have a duty to reduce suffering where we can we know that suffering is an inherent characteristic of life and it is beyond our capability to eliminate it all."

"Do not concern yourself, Augustus. I am sad, I can not deny that. But I am sad because I feel sorry for those poor people and not because I feel sorry for myself. And listening to your words I will be content if we can improve the lot of some of these poor wretches. I will not allow myself to be drawn into self-suffering because I understand the importance of attending to these poor souls."

"You have spoken wisely, Princess."

"Then what are we to do Augustus?"

"When we left the palace this morning, there were preparations being made for a large and rather extravagant feast. I know from my observations in recent months, that when such feasts are held there is much food left uneaten. What say we find some large baskets and fill them with the food that is left and take it to the poor tomorrow?"

The Princess seemed at once excited. "Do you think we could?"

"I see no reason why not. Most of the leftovers would either be thrown away or distributed among the occupants of the palace who surely are not in want of food. But they would make a big difference to some of those we saw today."

As they talked they were just leaving the more deprived areas of the city. But then a great commotion arose. Just in front of them a huge man appeared. His appearance was unkempt with knotted hair and a tangled beard. His clothes were torn and dirty. He was overturning tables where merchants had displayed their wares and flinging their produce hither and thither. He was obviously angry and shouting obscenities as he wrought his destruction. He was a little unsteady on his feet as though he may have been drinking. A couple of the traders in obvious terror cringed behind the remaining stalls. Others were fleeing into the street.

Hasim, concerned for his mistress's safety stepped forward with his hand on his scimitar. Augustus put his hand on Hasim's arm to constrain him, but not before the man had seen Hasim's tentative move forward. He snarled at Hasim, "So you young cur—you are spoiling for a fight, eh?"

"Wait, Hasim," Augustus cautioned.

Augustus strode forward and in a surprisingly loud voice, called, "Hoy, friend—whatever are you doing?"

The little Buddhist strode right up to the man and smiled. "You are making quite a mess you know."

Naomi was aghast at this turn of events and Hasim again moved forward to intervene.

Augustus noticing Hasim's approach called out, "No, Hasim—just let me talk a little while with my friend here."

"Friend? Friend? I don't have any friends," the man protested.

"Oh yes sir—indeed you do. I am concerned for you. Nobody causes destruction like this," Augustus continued waving his arms around at the scene of devastation, "unless he is exceedingly distressed. I want to know what distresses you."

"What concern would it be of yours little man? I should strike you for your impertinence."

"Well, I suppose you could try if you wanted to," said Augustus, "but I don't understand how that might make you feel any better. Tell me what ails you?"

Augustus bent down and restored a bench the man had overturned. He sat down and beckoned for the man to join him.

"If you can't tell me what ails you, can you at least tell me your name?" said Augustus. "My name is Augustus."

The man looked suspiciously at Augustus. "That is not a name I have heard before."

"I am not surprised," said Augustus. "It is not a name of these parts. But how are you called?"

The big fellow hesitated but seeing no obvious threat from the Buddhist he sat down on the other end of the bench. "I am called Doruk."

"Where are you from, Doruk?"

The big man bent over and placed his head in his hands.

"I come from the village of Bukrash which is to the North of here."

"What have you been drinking?"

This initially caused an angry reaction but when the man turned to Augustus and saw his open face with no sign of condemnation or criticism he sighed and said, "I have been drinking Raki."

"Ah, that's interesting. I don't drink but my father used to have sip of Raki each evening with my mother. In the evening when the weather was mild, after dinner they would sit on a bench under our apricot tree and partake of a small drink. They would discuss the issues of the day and he would put his arm around her as the evening got cooler. I have very fond memories of those times. It was marvelous to see the enduring love they had for each other. Tell me do you have a wife?"

The big man began to sob. Augustus put his hand consolingly on his shoulder. "What is it Doruk?"

Doruk just shook his head for a minute or two. Naomi, Hasim and some of the traders had heard the conversation and with Doruk now seemingly pacified, they came closer to hear more.

Finally Doruk looked up at Augustus. He wiped his face on his sleeve.

"I did have a wife," the big man said, "but she is gone."

The tears ran down his cheeks.

"I loved her so much. She was my life—and now she is gone I have nothing to live for."

But then he looked at Augustus accusingly. "But why am I telling you this, little man? This can be of no concern of yours. You are taking advantage of me."

Augustus put his arm around Doruk. "Oh no big fellow—this is a concern of mine. Every human being that suffers is a concern of mine. You won't understand this, but at a fundamental level, you and I are one. Every indignity you suffer hurts me as well. But how did you lose your wife?"

The tears streamed down his expansive face. He sobbed again for a few moments. Then he looked up at Augustus and said, "I lost her in childbirth. Both my wife and my daughter died that day. How can I go on living after that? If your young friend had withdrawn his scimitar and killed me here in the bazaar today, I would have been grateful."

"Then that would have been a huge waste and a great disaster."

"Why do you say that?"

"If you were killed you could not contribute to the world—and there is much more for you to do. If my young friend had slain you or even harmed you, he would have come to regret that. So let's be pleased that those things were averted. But tell me if you can, why did you vent your wrath here?"

"I know this will seem irrational to you, but this is where I came to buy my wedding ring when my relationship with my wife held such promise. And this is where I came to buy the essentials that my new child would need. What a fruitless effort that all turned out to be."

The traders now were righting their stalls and putting their produce back for display.

"I didn't come to attack these poor fellows. I actually came to look for some employment. But when I walked past the bazaar those memories came flooding back and I became incensed by what fate has done to me—it spat in my face just as I was on the cusp of great happiness."

Doruk looked around guiltily as the traders tried to restore their stalls and replace their produce.

"Here let me help you" Doruk said.

He moved to right the furniture and pick up the wares that had been displaced. The traders initially shrank back, their fear having been rekindled.

"Don't concern yourselves," Augustus called to them. "He will do you no harm."

Hasim came forward also and helped restore the stalls and their various goods on display. In ten minutes or so things were just as they had been previously.

Augustus rejoined the big man. Hasim and Naomi stood quietly near waiting for Augustus to be finished.

Doruk sighed. "I suppose I should learn not to drink so much Raki."

"Perhaps that would be useful," responded Augustus, "but it would be even more helpful if you learnt to control your emotions."

"And how can I do that," Doruk responded sceptically. "Do you have a magic wand that can take my sadness away?"

"No, of course not. But I can teach you a few things to improve your personal well-being and still your disturbed state of mind."

Doruk laughed derisively. "Oh, so then you are a magician."

He shook his head. "You seem such a nice little man and I was convinced that your concern for me was genuine, but now I am beginning to suspect that you are just another charlatan."

Naomi could constrain herself no longer. Stepping up closer she exclaimed, "Sir, I will have you know that Augustus is a great sage and a fine teacher. The very benefits he offers you he has already bestowed on me. I was stricken with great unhappiness to the degree that I could not function effectively in my life. Through his kind ministrations I have now become whole again, and although not completely cured of my affliction, am now living a largely happy and fulfilling life."

"And who are you madam, that you should give him such a ringing endorsement?"

"Who I am should not matter to you, but if it helps give my claims any credence then I should tell you I am Naomi, the daughter of the Sultan."

The big man shook his head in dismay. He looked Naomi directly in the eyes and said contritely, "I am sorry My Lady. I did not mean to offend. My apologies, Augustus. With such an endorsement I must know what it is I must do to gain your assistance."

"Well, big fellow, first I need to know what sort of employment you seek."

"I have a special gift (and I can assure you that I don't say this egotistically) with horses. My father bred and raised and sold horses. I inherited from him a small property near Bukrash. I had intended to follow in his footsteps with the enterprise. But once I lost my wife, I had no heart for it. But in short, if I could work with animals, particularly horses I would be greatly pleased."

"Well, we will bear that in mind and take whatever opportunity we can to find you such employment. But I would like to meet you again tomorrow and do a little work with you to help your state of mind."

Doruk sat and thought for a few moments. Then he looked up and smiled. "How could I decline an offer that has been recommended by a Princess?"

Naomi blushed.

But Augustus continued.

"You may have to do something in recompense."

"Well don't ask me for money, I have very little."

"I wouldn't think of asking you for money but we might like to take advantage of those big arms of yours."

"How so?"

"Well the Princess, Hasim and I are planning to go out into the city tomorrow and distribute food to the poor. Would you like to help? If you assist us that will be a considerably larger amount we could distribute. After the distribution I would be happy to sit and work with you."

Naomi and Hasim raised their eyebrows at this strange development.

Doruk mused a moment and then looked at Naomi. "Well, My Lady—is this a fair contract?"

Naomi recovered her composure very quickly "A more than fair contract Doruk. I know you will not regret it."

"Then so be it," the big man replied.

"Very well then," said Augustus, "meet us at the palace gates tomorrow morning and we will set out on this great endeavour."

Doruk nodded his assent. Augustus placed his arm on Doruk's shoulder. "Thank you for agreeing to help us," he said. "I look forward to seeing you tomorrow."

Hasim, Naomi and Augustus then made their way back to the palace. Nothing was said for a long time as the recent events went through their minds.

Finally the Princess asked, "Augustus, when you went forward to engage with Doruk, weren't you afraid? He was so much bigger than you and so aggressive when we first saw him."

Augustus laughed. "No Princess, I was not afraid. Why should I be? At the level of our principal essence he and I are one."

"That is a philosophical response Augustus. Surely he could have harmed you greatly."

"Well I suspect not, Princess. I am small but I have some useful physical skills my teachers have taught me. It would be unlikely anybody could do great physical harm to me. But that is not the point. When someone is overcome by anger, they are just deluded. They are punishing themselves and hoping that somehow that punishment might cause others to yield to their wishes."

"Anyhow," Naomi continued, "I am pleased no one was hurt. But tell me do you always offer your services to strangers?"

"I take what opportunity I can to ease the suffering of others. Remember you were a stranger to me also when I first came to the palace."

Naomi smiled and nodded. "That is indeed true."

On arriving at the palace the three (Naomi had somehow inveigled the bodyguard to be part of the plot) found some large wicker baskets and went to the banquet hall and filled them with food. In the Sultan's absence the Grand Vizier had hosted a group of visiting dignitaries. After the group had dined there was, as usual, a large amount of food remaining. There were pieces of bread, fruit and joints of meat that had not been finished. When the baskets were loaded, Augustus said, "Bring these to my room. I will take care of them and tomorrow we will distribute them among the poor."

CHAPTER 24

"Who is the happiest of men? He who values the merits
of others, and in their pleasure takes joy, even as though
'twere his own."

Johann Wolfgang von Goethe

The next day, after completing their morning practice, the Princess, the Buddhist and the bodyguard, met with Doruk at the palace gates. Doruk had tidied himself up and wore clean clothes. His beard had been trimmed and his hair cut.

Augustus winked at Naomi and said, "This does not seem to be the same rough fellow we met yesterday."

Doruk laughed. "I have never been in the presence of a Princess and a magician before. It seemed to me that I should be a little more respectful than I was yesterday."

They distributed the baskets among them, with Doruk and Hasim taking the heavier loads, and once more journeyed into the city. The baskets full of food were covered in linen so the people they passed could not see their contents. When they arrived in the poor quarter, they began handing out their booty. Children seemed to appear from every nook and cranny. Hasim was hard pressed to keep them at bay and maintain some order over the distribution process. They had almost emptied their baskets of their contents when Augustus said, "Wait. We must keep some for the lady at the olive grove." The Princess's face was flushed with excitement. It was apparent that she had enjoyed the role of beneficiary.

Then they hurried off to the olive grove, and just as they had requested the mother they had met there the previous day had returned.

Naomi quickly strode up to her. "How fare you this morning?"

The woman smiled. "I am well and most grateful for your generosity."

"Were you able to trade the jewellery and find food and lodging?"

"Yes, indeed! When I left you I took great care to trade the necklace as best I could. I took it to a number of traders in the bazaar. They initially offered me little for it, pretending I must have stolen it or trying to convince me it was a worthless ornament."

Basheer went on to relate how she had finally disposed of the necklace, find accommodation and go to the bazaar to buy some essentials for her child and herself.

"Since I saw you yesterday, my Lady—in a mere twenty four hours—my fortunes have soared. I can not know how to thank you. And here I have brought you the remainder of the money. I have all that I need now."

Naomi was overwhelmed. "No, please keep the money. You will need it before too long."

The Princess kissed the woman on the cheek and said, "May Allah be with you."

She turned and headed back to the palace with Augustus, Doruk and the bodyguard hurrying to catch up. When Augustus came up alongside, she smiled at him and said, "This, perhaps, has been the happiest day of my life."

"I am pleased for you, Princess, but remember that sadness will return. Just this time you are ready for it."

"I hope so—but no talk of clouds right now."

Augustus turned to the bodyguard and said, "Hasim will you escort the Princess to the palace? Now I must have a word with Doruk."

Hasim nodded and walked away with the Princess at his side.

Augustus and Doruk found a quiet place in the shade where they could sit and talk without undue interruption. Thus Augustus began his instruction of Doruk.

Later that evening Augustus and the Princess sat in the ante-room after completing their evening practice.

Naomi looked at Augustus and said, "Can we do again what we did today? There would be many little bellies with food in them tonight that otherwise would have been empty. I would really like to continue this work."

"I can see no reason why we can't Princess. Every time your father or his officials host a feast we can distribute the left-overs in this way."

"Good! I would like that."

"You have been very generous Princess. Now I would like to give you something. Wait here a moment."

Augustus got up and left the room. Naomi looked puzzled. She turned to Asma, who as usual was sitting in the rear sewing, and said, "I wonder what he is up to?"

Asma merely smiled and shrugged her shoulders.

In a few minutes Augustus returned. He carried with him the scroll in the wooden box that he had purchased in the bazaar on the day he first arrived at Yolanpur. "This, My Lady, is for you."

Naomi took the wooden box and opened it. She unrolled the scroll and read it.

> "Although you may attempt to do a hundred things in this world, only Love will give you release from the bondage of yourself."
>
> Jami
> (poet of Persia, saint and mystic)

She looked inquiringly at Augustus. "Why have you given me this?"

"Isn't it obvious? Today your love freed you from the bondage of yourself. It is always thus. When you can forget yourself, life becomes much easier. The easiest way to forget yourself is to be concerned for others. You have been considerate of the poor of your city. You should feel some satisfaction from that. You are indeed a person who can make a difference. You can not now say that you are unworthy. You have shown your worth by your concern for others and the practical help you have given them. It is true that we did not feed all the poor. It is true that many of them may be hungry again tomorrow. But we did what we could do. Be content with that."

"Oh, Augustus, how wise you are! I will indeed be content this evening. And how easy will it be to do my affirmations. All the positive things that have happened today will be enough to sustain me for a long, long time. But before you go this evening, can I ask something of you?"

"Of course, My Lady. What is your concern?"

"I am feeling a little guilty Augustus. I got great joy in helping those poor people today. I am beginning to wonder whether I did it for their benefit or whether I did it for mine. Is this just another form of selfishness on my part that I should want to help the poor because it gives me joy?"

"That is an interesting question, Princess. However you should not concern yourself. I know that you went into the city today because you were motivated to help the poor. The goodness of your act is not diminished because it gave you joy as well. Let me put it this way. If a farmer sets out to grow some wheat, his intention is to harvest the grain. But when he harvests his wheat not only does he get grain but he gets straw as well. The straw he harvests is a natural byproduct of growing wheat. It is a wonderful characteristic of altruism that when you sow compassion you not only harvest a reduction in suffering of others but you also harvest personal joy."

The Princess nodded her understanding. "Thank you Augustus. The only thing that would now make my happiness complete would be to go to that special place you have been promising to take me to."

"Do not worry Princess. The time is fast approaching when we might enter there."

CHAPTER 25

"It is important to expect nothing, to take every
experience, including the negative ones, as merely steps
on the path, and to proceed."

Ram Dass

Now in the mornings, after he had attended to the Princess, Augustus would leave the palace and meet with Doruk. He found to his initial surprise that Doruk was a very good pupil. Together they explored the meditation practice, an understanding of awareness, the importance of a constructive world view, as well as altruism and compassion.

Augustus spent some time elaborating about the problems of attachment.

"No doubt," he said, "you had a very special relationship with your wife. And no doubt you had great affection for her. But let me say that despite your love for her, you can be happy without her."

"You do not understand, Augustus. She was my life. I can not imagine happiness without her,"

"It is admirable," said Augustus, "that you should hold her memory so dear. Be grateful that you should have had such a wonderful relationship. But she is gone and life must go on. I do not say this with disrespect for your wife. I have no doubt she was a wonderful person. But you are vulnerable every time you believe that your happiness is dependant on anything else but your own concept of mind or your own concept of the world."

As the weeks went by Doruk's understanding grew, as did his sense of equanimity.

One morning, Augustus appeared at the palace gates accompanied by Naomi and her bodyguard.

"Doruk," said Augustus, "the Princess has requested that I accompany her to see a young woman for whom we have concerns. She is being accommodated at an inn of the far side of town. If you wish to accompany us, you and I can further our practice as we walk. If that is not a suitable arrangement, we will have to postpone our usual session until tomorrow morning."

"Oh, no, Augustus it would be a privilege to walk with you and the Princess and even with the young man who would have cut my head off," he said winking at Hasim.

Then he turned to Naomi and in a more serious voice, said. "I am very grateful my Lady, that you saw fit to recommend your little magician to me. He has been most helpful.'

"I am pleased Doruk because he has been most helpful to me as well. But let us now go and see Basheera."

The Princess turned and with Hasim at her side marched off. She felt it appropriate that she should leave a space for Augustus and Doruk to talk as they walked. The Grand Vizier had given her directions on how to get to Ishmael's inn and she was curious to know how Basheer and her daughter were now faring. Augustus and Doruk followed chatting all the while some ten metres behind. Augustus gave Doruk some insights into mindfulness as they walked.

Finally they arrived at the inn. Ishmael, seeing the four figures approaching, came out to meet them.

"What can I do for you, my friends? I hope you are not seeking accommodation for all our rooms are occupied."

Naomi stepped forward. "Are you the one called Ishmael?" she asked.

"That is my name."

"Then I come here under instruction from Abdullah, the Sultan's Grand Vizier to enquire after the welfare of Basheera and her daughter."

"Well, I certainly have a friend called Abdullah. But who might you be asking after one of my guests? I wish no offence, but I have obligations to those that I accommodate; I will not give out information unless I am sure it is not contrary to their welfare."

Naomi smiled. Ishmael seemed to be such a principled man. She was glad that Abdullah had entrusted Basheer to him.

"Do not concern yourself Ishmael. I am the Princess Naomi. I gave Basheer a necklace to trade so that she would have succour for herself and her child. It is my desire to know how she fares. I was so concerned for her and her child and I would sleep better if I knew she was well and properly cared for."

Ishmael pondered awhile. But before long he came to the conclusion that for someone to know of these circumstances, which surely few could have known, Naomi must have been speaking the truth.

"I am sorry My Lady, I meant no offence. But I had to be sure that I did not compromise Basheer. I will go and get her for you. This way you can hear first hand how she fares."

Naomi smiled.

"Thank you Ishmael. I now see why our wise friend entrusted her to you."

Ishmael bowed slightly. "Thank you, Princess. If you wait here I will bring her to you shortly."

The little group of four waited patiently at the inn door. But true to his word, within a minute or two Ishmael returned with Basheer in tow. But when Basheer saw the Princess she ran forward and embraced her.

Naomi held her close. But after a little while put her hands on Basheer's shoulders and looked into her face.

"It is so good to see you Basheer. I have been wondering for some time how you have fared. I felt compelled to come and see you."

"You need not concern yourself, Princess. This man," she said turning to Ishmael, "and his adorable wife have made me and my daughter feel as though we have a new family. They have attended to our every need. How fortunate was I to have met you and then been guided by Abdullah so that I was introduced into their household. When I lost my husband I did not think that I could be happy again. Whilst I miss my husband greatly, I have learnt that I can still be happy. But that realisation would never have occurred without your generosity."

Again, she hugged the Princess.

Doruk listened intently to the conversation. Maybe he, whilst always honouring his love for her, could also be happy without his wife.

They were all standing in the street at the entrance to the inn. On the road behind them came a cart, pulled by a large white horse. The cart was loaded with pottery. It was easy to see that the horse was struggling. Finally exhausted, the mare stopped in the middle of the road. The potter walking alongside was angry that the poor beast was not progressing as he would like. He raised a switch which he had broken from a tree earlier and thrashed the horse's flank. He cursed the horse for its intransigence and raised his arm again to repeat the punishment. The horse whinnied in fear.

Doruk ran forward and grabbed the potter's arm.

"Don't harm her," he said. He spoke not loudly but with a steely determination. "This is an old horse and your load is severely taxing her."

The potter struggled with Doruk trying to withdraw his arm but Doruk's size and his strength rendered it an unequal contest. Doruk dragged the switch from the man's clutches and broke into pieces which he flung on to the ground.

Then without anger he turned and smiled at the potter. "You must learn to manage your animal in a gentler way."

He turned to the horse and walked up to the poor quivering beast. He stroked the horse and talked gently to it.

Finally, he turned back to the potter.

"Where are you taking your load sir? I will help you there."

The potter was bemused by this turn of events. Whilst because of his size Doruk was very imposing, because of his calm demeanour he was not threatening.

"I need to take my wares to the bazaar. This is my livelihood. If I can't sell my wares, I can't support my family."

Doruk nodded. He stroked the horse's head and whispered gently in its ear. Then he led the beast away towards the bazaar. The horse followed willingly and the potter walked in the rear shaking his head.

As he led the horse, Doruk called back to Augustus, "I will see you back at the palace gates in an hour. Does that suit you?"

Augustus smiled, "Yes my big friend—that sounds fine. Just take care not to hurt anybody."

Doruk laughed. "Have no fear of that, my little magician."

The little group in front of the inn had watched intently what had transpired.

Basheer was the first to comment. "What a fine man that he should intervene to prevent the horse suffering!"

"Indeed," said Ishmael. "Augustus, it seems as though your large friend has some talent with animals."

"Well, yes, Ishmael. I suspect he does."

"Well I soon will travel into the provinces to ply my trade. I have a couple of horses and a wagon. But I have little expertise myself with animals. I wonder if he would like to accompany me. I would of course pay him. He is also a rather imposing fellow. I am a goldsmith and I carry materials of some value when I travel. I am sure his presence might deter would-be thieves as well which would be helpful. I intend to take Basheer and her daughter with me to reunite them with their relatives. I would feel more at ease if I had someone to help me protect their welfare. Is he trustworthy?"

"That is an intriguing offer Ishmael. I suspect Doruk might be interested. I will put it to him when I see him later. If he is so inclined I will get him to come to you and discuss the details of your arrangement. As to his trustworthiness, I have but known him a month or two, but I feel confident that he will now not let you down."

"Thank you, Augustus. I would appreciate that."

Later, after meeting again at the palace gates, at Augustus's instigation, Doruk went to see Ishmael.

"Augustus has told me you wish me to accompany you on a journey?" he enquired of the goldsmith.

"Yes, Doruk. I travel North several times a year to do commerce in a number of the townships in that region. I am a goldsmith and my wares are quite valuable. What's more I have promised Basheer I would take her and her daughter with me to rejoin relatives. Now I am getting older and not as robust as I used to be. I would like some help in tending the horses that draw my wagon. I would also appreciate someone to help me guard my wares and to ensure the welfare of Basheer and her daughter. You seemed to me a likely candidate. You have some skill with horses and you are a sturdy fellow and your presence would help deter thieves and other miscreants we might meet. Our track takes us through some wild places where sometimes undesirables are said to lurk. I would of course recompense you for this."

Doruk mused on the proposition for a while. He enjoyed working with horses—so that was an attractive proposition. His heart stirred for Basheer and her child. Her loss resonated with him. What's more he felt a strange attraction to her that was due to more than their shared circumstances.

He looked up and smiled at Ishmael.

"Thank you for your offer sir. I would be pleased to accept."

The old goldsmith shook Doruk's hand and then embraced him.

"I am so pleased, big fellow, that you will join us. I feel more secure about Basheer's welfare not to mention my wares."

They stood and talked awhile and Doruk agreed on the conditions of his employ. Ishmael told him when they would set off and what to bring with him.

Lightheartedly, Doruk walked back to the palace to tell Augustus about his assignment.

CHAPTER 26

"There is a wonderful mythical law of nature that the
three things we crave most in life—happiness, freedom,
and peace of mind—are always attained by giving them to
someone else."

Peyton Conway March

The weeks went by, and Augustus, the Princess, her bodyguard and Doruk went many times into the city with food for the poor. The Princess was getting to be well-known by the city folk and they would call out their blessings as she walked among them. She was loved by the children and she could usually find something for each of the neediest. She was very happy.

Then one evening, Augustus and the Princess were meditating as was their wont. They had been engaged in their practice for at least a half hour. Suddenly, a court attendant, burst in and said, "Princess, your father has returned and would talk with you."

Naomi roused herself from her meditation and said, "Very well, I will go to him with your blessing Augustus."

"Of course My Lady. I hope you enjoy your reuniting with your father."

She had missed her father during his absence and she was keen to tell him of the wonderful things that had happened while he was away. She arose from her meditation position and headed off to the throne room.

Augustus was intrigued by these developments and followed her.

When she reached the throne room, Naomi adopted a posture of humility and went and kneeled before her father. "Sire, you have sent for me. What is it that I can do for you?"

The Sultan looked at his daughter with a puzzled look on his face. "Naomi, my dear, I recently gave you a necklace in appreciation of your improved disposition and to acknowledge my great love for you. Abdullah has retrieved this necklace from a woman at the bazaar. He recognised it as the necklace I gave you and restored it to me."

The Princess began to cry. "Oh father, I am so ashamed that I should have given away the gift you gave me. I am so unworthy of your love!"

The Sultan was nonplussed by this response. "Oh no, Naomi—do not believe that there is any concern about what you did with my gift. A gift given in good faith surely is delivered to someone to do whatsoever they will with it. I was just concerned for you and confused when your necklace was brought to me."

"If my gift were to have provisos or terms, then it would not be a gift at all. If I give something to you, but only on the basis that you give something back to me, that is not a gift. That is plain commerce. Or if I give you something but put constraints on what you should do with it, that is not a gift either. My love of you is such a gift. I do not give it with conditions. There is nothing you need do to earn it. And, indeed, there is nothing you could do to lose it. My love of you is unconditional."

"Consequently, I have no concern about what you did with the necklace. Abdullah told me the story of the woman to whom you gave the necklace and her sorry state. It was an act of great generosity to give her the necklace. I gave it to you but because it was a gift, an unconditional gift, what you did with it was entirely up to you. In fact I am proud of you and your generosity."

"Here, let me return the jewellery to you again to adorn your pretty neck." He lifted the necklace over her head and straightened it on her throat. Then he kissed her. "I am indeed blessed to have a daughter who is so generous."

Naomi hugged him in return and the tears that now made their way down her cheeks were tears of joy.

The Sultan continued, "But tell me my girl, what is it that you have been doing out in the city with Augustus."

Naomi was about to speak but Augustus intervened before she could utter a word. "Allow me, sire, to explain. Each of us, as individuals, have our particular strengths and qualities that we benefit from exercising. It helps our sense of self, strengthens our psychological robustness and contributes to our well-being to be able to utilise these characteristics. The two such strengths I have found in your daughter are her passion for music and her generosity. For some time now, we have ensured that she plays her flute every day and that has been quite therapeutic for her. Just lately we have sought an outlet for her generosity and her empathy. It was not appropriate to do this earlier. We first had to find respite for your daughter from her own suffering. When you are engrossed in your own suffering you are normally oblivious to the suffering of others. Once the Princess's equilibrium was restored she was awakened to the plight of the poor in your city. When there is a feast in the palace, it has become our habit to collect the left over food and distribute it to the poor. This too brings joy to the Princess. It has also served to put a sense of meaning and purpose back into the Princess's life. She has a need to serve and care for your people. Our sojourns into the city to feed the poor have provided her with a practical way of meeting that need. It was on one such visit that we came across the woman, Basheer and her child."

Naomi looked anxiously at her father as he took in Augustus's words. She was relieved when he smiled and nodded. "That is a good and generous thing to do. I tend to overfeed my guests and they are not generally in as much need as those who have benefited by their left-overs! Would you permit that I should come with you some time in the future?"

Augustus looked at the Princess for her response. "Of course, Father. I would enjoy having you come along as well."

"I am happy for you and Augustus to pursue your little enterprise for the time being, but perhaps if you could remind me in a month or two I shall certainly make the effort to join you on your mission of mercy."

"Very well," said the Princess. "I will look forward to it!"

CHAPTER 27

"We shall not cease from exploration
And the end of all our exploring
Will be to arrive where we started
And know the place for the first time"

T. S. Eliot

They had been on the road for many hours. Now the sun was starting to set.

Ishmael said to Doruk, "We need to find somewhere to stay for the night."

"I know these parts reasonably well, Ishmael. We are only five minutes away from a little stream with some lovely shade trees where we could stay comfortably for the night."

"Very well. Let us make our way there and then set up camp for the evening."

Shortly afterwards they arrived at a sheltered spot and pulled the cart up under a large shady tree. They disembarked the cart. Doruk unhitched the horses and led them to the creek to drink. He then tethered them with a long rope each so that they could continue to graze on the lush grass at the stream's edge.

Ishmael was unpacking their bedding and cooking utensils from the cart as Doruk returned. He took a couple of pails from the cart and went back to the stream to fill them.

Ishmael turned to Basheer. "Would you like to take your daughter down to the water and wash off a little grime?"

"That would be pleasant, thank you Ishmael."

"Good. I will stay here and guard our possessions and continue making camp until you return."

"And I," added Doruk, "will go and gather some firewood".

He pointed to his left. "I will go this way down the stream to gather wood. If you go the other way you will find a sandy bank which allows you easy access to the water. That way I won't intrude on you whilst you perform your ablutions."

Doruk headed off to gather wood.

He contemplated on his journey so far. Ishmael had stopped by a couple of villages and sold a few pieces to traders there. He had seemed pleased with the outcome. Ishmael was a canny negotiator but not greedy. And he took great care to protect his wares. He was careful not to show all his wares at once which might have attracted too much attention and raised the interest of would-be thieves. He had a special hiding place in the wagon for his chest of crafted gold pieces. He had constructed a compartment under the floor of the wagon that wasn't visible from the top or the sides. The door to the secret compartment was locked and he carried the key to the lock in a small leather holder on his belt. He wore this at his back so that it was not readily visible to others.

Doruk could not believe how his life had changed in recent times. When Augustus had first encountered him, he was bitter and angry. Augustus's instruction had certainly helped him restore some equanimity. And he had enjoyed working with Ishmael. The old man was kind and wise. Helping him along the way and caring for the horses had brought a sense of fulfillment greater than he had experienced for some time.

But as he foraged for firewood he could not avoid the realisation that his new-found happiness was somehow due to Basheer. He was almost ashamed to admit that he had met somebody who was attractive to him as his wife had been. Initially that realisation came with some guilt.

There on the ground in front of him was a nice piece of hardwood. That was what he was looking for. It would be good to light a fire whose embers were still fresh in the morning so that it could be rekindled. He picked it up and cradled it in the crook of his arm.

They had talked many times during the journey. She enquired after his circumstances and tears welled in her eyes when he told of his wife's death. She said very little about her husband but he could see her private memories were still painful and he did not press her for fear of reigniting painful memories.

But it had been a source of great delight to him to have bonded with Basheer's daughter, Azize. After a couple of days of travelling when he would bring her flowers which he had plucked from the side of the road, or pointed out to her birds whose beauty and songs caused her to laugh with appreciation, they grew close. In the evenings she would come and sit on his lap and he would tell her folk stories from his tradition which she found intriguing.

"This is the daughter that I almost had," he thought to himself.

And when he retired he lay on his makeshift bed and the tears welled in his eyes when he remembered his wife and the daughter he had lost. But after a time he found he could smile when he thought of this beautiful child and her beautiful mother that had become his privilege to accompany.

As he foraged for wood he found another limb off a hardwood tree. It was a little long but Ishmael had an axe in the wagon and he could chop it into reasonable sized pieces when he got back to the camp.

Basheer sat by the water's side and watched while her daughter splashed and played in the little stream. She felt so grateful to see Azize so happy. When she thought back about the last couple of weeks her head spun. She was so pleased to be journeying to meet her family members and thought how joyous it would be to be with them again.

But now she wished that the journey would not end. How wonderful it had been. Ishmael had been kind and concerned for their welfare and she would always be grateful to him. But this great bear of a man who had accompanied them as well, had wangled his way into their hearts. He was such a big man and yet he was so gentle. She smiled when she thought of how he would cradle Azize in his arms after the day's end. He would stroke her lustrous hair and tell her stories. And during the day he always found something to amuse her. Her eyes glistened with tears when she thought that this was the role her loving husband would have played. But it was so nice to have a man show such affection to her daughter and be so kind and considerate to herself as well. She was confused. She knew she would always love her husband but could she find it in herself to allow this latent feeling of affection express itself for another man?

Finally she called to her daughter, "Azize, come and be dressed now. We must go back and help the men with supper."

The little girl came reluctantly back to the sandy bank where her mother dried her off and dressed her. Feeling refreshed and restored they turned to go back to the camp that Ishmael was preparing.

"Mama," asked the little girl, "do you think Doruk will tell me a story again this evening?"

"Would you like that?"

"Oh yes! He tells such funny stories!"

Basheer smiled. "Well I suspect he might if you ask him nicely."

CHAPTER 28

"Are you ready to cut off your head and place your foot
on it? If so, come; Love awaits you! Love is not grown in
a garden, nor sold in the marketplace; whether you are a
king or a servant, the price is your head, and nothing less."
Abu Hamid Al-Ghazzali

Sheltered by the thick undergrowth, the two men lay on the ground resting. They had had an exhausting but reasonably profitable day.

One raised himself to his haunches and addressed the other. He was a little wiry fellow with a gaunt face and long fingers. "Come Erkman, let us examine today's profits."

The other, a burlier man, yawned and looked up at his accomplice. "Habib, you can count. You don't need me to help you."

"All right, you sloth. I will do it for you."

He reached over to the untidy pile of clothing, utensils and bedding and grabbed a small bag. He was about to turn its contents out on the ground to count when he stopped abruptly.

"What's the matter, you little weasel?"

"Listen," the little fellow said with his fingers to his lips.

They both sat still. And sure enough there was the "clip-clop" of horses' hooves and the repetitive sound of wagon wheels impacting on the earth.

Erkman smiled. "Well, little fellow, perhaps we have a new benefactor."

As they listened the wagon seemed to have passed them. Habib got a little agitated. "We can't let them get away."

Erkman laughed. "They won't be going far at this time of evening."

Even as he spoke the sound of the horses slowed.

"See, I told you so. They will more than likely make camp by the stream. We'll let them get settled and then perhaps invite them to share their wealth with us!"

The two miscreants were close enough to hear the voices of the travellers, the horses whinnying and the sounds of the wagon being unloaded. Eventually, as the light faded, they decided to approach their prey. They stealthily made their way through the sparse undergrowth using the cover provided by the trees by the stream. Erkman held a long-bladed knife and Habib was similarly armed but his weapon was sheathed in a scabbard attached to his belt. As they approached the wagon they saw Basheer and Azize returning from the stream.

"Oh, what good luck this is," Erkman whispered to Habib. "Here we have two innocents at our mercy. That must surely provide us bargaining power over the owners of the wagon."

They managed to get themselves a little in front of the woman and her daughter and hid behind a large tree only about fifty metres from the cart. Basheer and Azize, unaware of the threat to them ambled back to the wagon in good spirits.

Waiting until the woman and her child had approached quite closely to the tree, the robbers sprang from their cover. Basheer screamed but Erkman was too quick and seized her from behind and held her tightly. Azize turned and went to flee. "Doruk! Doruk!" she called in a frightened shrill voice. But Habib caught her easily and covered her mouth with his hand.

Ishmael heard the commotion and looking up to find the men accosting Basheer and Azize, scurried down to their aid as fast as his old legs would allow.

"Unhand them," he called in a surprisingly strong voice.

But as he approached, Erkman held his knife out in front of Basheer so the old man could see it clearly, then turning it, placed the flat of the blade across Basheer's fair neck.

"Just stop right there, old man," Erkman commanded.

Ishmael stopped in his tracks. He had no wish to see Basheer harmed in any way. There seemed little he could do without putting Basheer and Azize at risk. Perhaps if he could delay proceedings long enough for Doruk to return things might be different.

"What do you want, you cowards!" the old man demanded.

"Nothing much," enjoined Habib with an evil laugh. "Only your money!"

"Well, that is settled then. You can have my money if you free the woman and the child."

"First we need to see your money," demanded Erkman.

"Come back to the camp and I will get it for you," said Ishmael. He turned and went as if to march back to the cart.

He had only gone but a few steps when he fell to the ground moaning.

"Get up! Get up, old man," screamed Habib.

Ishmael lay prostrate on the grass and continued to moan.

"I'll fix you," the little man cried out.

He ran forward but in doing so he had released his grip on Azize and she fled into the undergrowth.

He was about to give chase when Erkman said, "Don't concern yourself, friend. We don't need her as long as we have this one." He nodded towards Basheer.

Ishmael had now got up on his hands and legs. "Oh, I don't know what came over me. I had such a pain in my chest that I thought I might die."

Basheer started to cry.

"Leave him alone," she sobbed. "How can you harm a defenseless old man?"

There was a noise in the background of a twig snapping. Erkman and Habib looked at each other.

"Don't be concerned, it is only the girl, "Erkman said.

While they were so distracted Basheer looked at Ishmael. The old man winked at her. She immediately knew that he was well and all this was a subterfuge. If only Doruk would come.

CHAPTER 29

"What lies behind us, and what lies before us are tiny
matters compared to what lies within us."
Ralph Waldo Emerson ~

In the meantime, Doruk had now gathered up an armful of wood—
more than sufficient to light a cooking fire for the evening and to
restore it again in the morning. He was just about to return to the cart
when he came across a pile of disorderly chattels that seemed to indicate
someone had made a makeshift camp. He looked around but there was
no one to be seen. He had been told that there were some rough people
in these regions and there were tales of robbers who preyed on innocent
travellers. There was a little bag on the ground. He picked it up and
opened it and was surprised to see it was full of gold coins. Were the
occupants of the camp robbers? It seemed likely this was the case. He
was starting to feel some concern for those he had left.

He was about to put the bag down when he heard a woman's
scream. His heart beat fast. It must have come from Basheer! Surely
there were no other women in the vicinity. And then came the plaintive
shrill call, "Doruk! Doruk!" And that could only have been Azize.
Without thinking he thrust the bag of coins into his tunic pocket. He
dropped his load of wood, and was about to run back to the cart. But
he stopped momentarily and picked up again the longer tree limb he
had been carrying before rushing off.

He was in two minds what to do. His initial reaction was to get
back as fast as he could to protect those that he loved. But he realised if

he were to precipitately rush back he may be putting his little band at further risk. Consequently he ran back quickly until he was close and then approached the camp furtively.

As he progressed silently from tree to tree to close proximity he became aware of a quiet sobbing. He sought out the source of the noise and was surprised to see little Azize lying on the ground in the undergrowth. He ran forward towards her. She seemed to hear his approach and when she saw who it was she raised herself and was about to speak.

"Hush, little one, Doruk said quietly. "You are safe now."

He gathered the girl into his arms and hugged her tightly.

"Talk softly now and tell me what has happened."

The frightened little girl told him her story interspersed with sobs.

He kissed her gently and said, "Be very quiet. Have no fear for your mother. I will save her."

He said this so confidently that Azize stopped her crying and held him tightly.Doruk was outwardly calm but underneath was in a turmoil about how he might honour such an undertaking.

"Stay here," he whispered. "I will go and deal with these people, then I will come back for you."

Azize nodded. "Please don't let them harm Mama."

"Never fear. I will bring her safely back to you—I promise."

He wanted so much to be true to his word, and was keen not to reflect his doubts. He crept forward in the fading light until he was a mere ten metres from the group. He crouched behind a bush still carrying the tree limb.

Habib had turned his attention to Ishmael. "Come old man get your money out. When our hands are full of gold we won't be able to restrain the young lady."

Ishmael went to rummage through his belongings to find the money he had obtained for the trading of his wares.

"Don't stall, old man. My friend is very nervous. He could easily slip and cut the woman. Here let me help you," said Habib. As he approached Ishmael was bending over his possessions in the back of the cart. As he did so his tunic came up above his waist and exposed the leather wallet attached to his belt.

"Ah! That's where your money is," he shouted triumphantly placing his hand on the old man's waist.

But Ishmael stood his ground. "There is no money there," he said truthfully. "But I have some gold coins in a small bag here somewhere."

He continued to rummage through his things.

Doruk was alarmed by this turn of events. If the thieves discovered Ishmael's key they would not rest until they'd found his cache of gold craft. He decided it was time to act.

Because they were distracted by Ishmael's search Habib and Erkman did not notice Doruk's approach. He was quite close when he said in a loud, firm voice. "Stop. I will give you gold for the release of the lady."

In alarm the two miscreants turned to be confronted by Doruk's huge figure. As they did so he withdrew the bag of gold he had picked up at the campsite from his tunic pocket and threw it on the ground at his feet.

Habib recognised the bag and said, "But that is our bag of gold. You can't buy this woman's freedom with our own money! It is not yours to trade!"

Doruk, strangely, felt quite calm now. He laughed. "Well that woman is my dear friend and she is not yours to trade either. And if you harm her in any way, you will regret it."

Basheer's heart lit up. She was confident that Doruk would save them. But perhaps she could help. Erkman turned to confront Doruk taking the blade away from Basheer's throat. As soon as he did so Basheer struck him a blow in his lower stomach with her clenched fist. Erkman stumbled and Basheer fled and stood behind Doruk.

"Well done, Basheer," said Doruk. He didn't take his gaze away from the robbers as he talked. "Go now and attend Azize. She is in the bushes behind me—perhaps fifty metres away."

Basheer ran off into the undergrowth calling, "Azize, Azize!"

Ishmael had taken advantage of the distraction also. He had run to the back of the cart and picked up his axe. He took his belt off and threw it and the pouch containing the key to his cache into the undergrowth while the two were distracted.

Doruk confronted Erkman.

"Throw down your knife. Take your money and go."

But Erkman was having none of it.

"I don't think so, big fellow. The old man has more to give yet. And you don't frighten me. I have my knife and it has cut many men and even some as big as you. A big oaf with a stick is no match for me and my knife."

Doruk sighed. "I don't want to hurt you but I will do everything I can to protect my friends and their possessions. Just throw the knife down and recover your bag of ill-gotten gains and be off."

Habib was cowering with his back to the wagon. "Do as he says Erkman. We lose nothing if you take his offer."

"You little cur! Have some courage. Are you going to back down every time some oaf confronts you? It is time for you to make a concession big man," he said turning to Doruk. "Give me the old man's money and I won't cut you."

Doruk sighed. "You leave me no choice."

The big man moved forward. The robber lunged with his knife. Doruk averted the thrust which was aimed at his stomach with the stick he carried. The knife slid off the tree limb and cut through the sleeve of his tunic. But the momentum carried Erkman past him and turning, Doruk struck him heavily on his right forearm. It seemed as if the blow had broken Erkman's arm. He screamed and dropped the knife. Erkman backed away holding his arm. Doruk picked up the knife. He turned then to Habib.

"Throw your knife on the ground also little man."

Doruk stood over him menacingly with his stick raised. Habib was terrified and quickly undid his belt and threw it with the scabbard and knife onto the ground at Doruk's feet.

"Now pick up your bag and be gone, both of you. If I should see you again be sure you won't escape so lightly."

Habib snatched the bag up off the ground and the two robbers scuttled off into the night with Erkman moaning and groaning and cradling his injured arm.

Ishmael came up and embraced Doruk.

"Well, big fellow, you have certainly earned your keep this evening. Thank you for your courage."

"I am pleased to have been able to help, my friend. We can't let scoundrels like those interfere with honest folk like you and Basheer."

Soon after, Basheer and Azize appeared. They had crept forward to see what was happening. Basheer could not restrain herself. She rushed forward and embraced Doruk.

"Thank you Doruk. You have saved us from the robbers."

Doruk was taken aback. He was so overwhelmed by Basheer's response. He was overcome by her gratitude. He loved the warmth of her pressing herself against him.

Azize hugged his huge leg—she could not reach any further. "You have saved my Mama as you said you would. Oh how I love you!"

The big fellow smiled and hoisted her up. "And I love you also little princess. Let us prepare a meal and then perhaps if you are willing, I will tell you a story."

"Oh, yes please—I love your stories!"

But then Basheer said, "You are bleeding. Are you all right?"

"Yes Basheer, I am fine. When I fended away the robber's knife it sliced through the sleeve of my tunic and cut my upper arm. But it is of no import."

But Basheer was not to be put off. "Oh, you poor man—you have suffered this wound in protecting us. Let me tend to it for you."

She cajoled the big man into taking off his tunic. She manufactured a bandage and found some ointment and dressed the wound. In truth Doruk had no concern about his cut but rather enjoyed the attention that Basheer lavished on him.

After she had dressed his wound Doruk started a small fire. Basheer set about cooking a meal for them. They were amply provisioned, having replenished their supplies at the last village. Ishmael tidied up the camp site and arranged their bedding. While Basheer cooked, Doruk told Azize a story and she was soon laughing and chortling in delight. Soon after they had eaten they retired. Whilst Doruk was reasonably sure they wouldn't be bothered again by the robbers he nevertheless slept with Erkman's long knife alongside him. He slept fitfully awakening frequently and listening carefully to the sounds around about. But the night went by without incident and he was relieved when finally it was dawn.

CHAPTER 30

"Life is like riding a bicycle. To keep your balance you must keep moving."

Albert Einstein

The Princess Naomi and Augustus had gone to see Ishmael. They had heard of his return and wanted to know how Basheer had fared. When they got to the inn they found Ishmael, Lateefah and Doruk in the little courtyard at the rear of the building.

'Well, Ishmael," enquired Augustus, "how did the journey go? Did you deliver Basheer safely to her family?"

"We did indeed, Augustus. But in the end I suspect she was just a little disappointed to be there?"

Naomi seemed intrigued by this statement. "Why would that be, Ishmael?" she asked. "She seemed keen to be restored to her family."

Ishmael smiled. Turning to Doruk, he said, "I think it was because over the course of our journey she seemed to develop a certain fondness for this big fellow."

"I am intrigued now," she responded. "Tell me Doruk, what have you been up to?"

Doruk blushed.

"To tell the truth, Princess, I did very little. But whilst we travelled together I got to know Basheer better and found her to be a wonderful woman. I also grew very fond of her daughter, Azize. Basheer has many of the fine qualities of my poor deceased wife, and Azize reminded me of the daughter I wished we could have raised."

"He is very humble, My Lady when he says he did very little. In fact he saved us from robbers who would have stolen our goods and might have done us physical harm. He was a marvellous travelling companion, helping wherever he could, tending the horses well and displayed great courage in protecting us. If he were to stay I'd be happy to have him permanently in my employ."

"What do you mean, 'if he were to stay'?" enquired the Princess, now even further intrigued.

Ishmael turned to Doruk who looked down bashfully.

"Well, tell them, Doruk—they are your friends," urged the old man.

"They are indeed Ishmael. Augustus has been so good to me and in many ways helped to get my life back in order. And I enjoyed going with the Princess to help the poor in the city."

He looked Naomi directly in the eye. "I have asked Basheer to marry me, and she has agreed. I told her I had to honour my undertaking to Ishmael to see him safely home but that as soon as I was able I would come for her. I plan to set out tomorrow."

Naomi clapped her hands in delight.

"How wonderful!" she cried and ran forward and hugged him. "I am so pleased for you both."

"Thank you," said Doruk humbly but with genuine gratitude.

"To add to my joy, my old friend here," he said turning to Ishmael, "has fashioned a fine ring for my bride to be."

"It was the least I could do considering you saved us from the robbers."

"May we see it?" Naomi enquired.

"Certainly," said Ishmael.

He disappeared inside and soon came out with a little velvet bag tied with a yellow sash. He unfastened the neck of the bag and tipped its contents onto his hand. He stretched his hand out to Naomi. "Here it is!"

The Princess picked it up and fingered it gently. "Why, that is beautiful, Ishmael. Your bride will be well-pleased with this, Doruk."

"I am sure she will my lady. It is a fine ring created by a fine craftsman. But tell me princess do you still distribute food to the needy in the city?"

"Indeed I do Doruk. And I have to confess to you that our sorties into the poor areas of the city give me great satisfaction. Surprisingly, my father, the Sultan, wishes to come with me as well to give food to the needy. He has asked that he should accompany me the next time we go forth to feed the poor."

"I will not be able to accompany you my lady, for I shall be gone in the morning, but I would love to have been able to go with you again. Tell me when will you go forth with your father?"

The princess responded, "It would seem to be the day after tomorrow. I am excited at the prospect."

CHAPTER 31

"Society comprises two classes: those who have more food
than appetite, and those who have more appetite than
food."
Sébastien-Roch Nicholas de Chamfort

On the appointed day, the Sultan accompanied Naomi and Augustus
into the slums. In order not to create a spectacle, he had put on the
clothes of a peasant and carried one of the baskets of food. He had not
told any of his court about his planned foray into the city. He knew
they would have fussed and implored him to take bodyguards to protect
his person. But he wanted none of that, determined to see things just
as they were.

Thus they set off, the Sultan, the Princess, Augustus and Hasim.
The Sultan was dismayed by the sight of so many poor people. He had
been unaware, as the Grand Vizier had noted, of their plight so close
to his sumptuous abode. The benefactors distributed their bounty and
returned to the palace. Very little was said because they could see the
Sultan was preoccupied in thought. As they arrived at the Palace gates
the Sultan turned and said to his daughter, "Princess, you are indeed a
wondrous person to have such compassion. I was unaware of the amount
of suffering that existed here right on my own doorstep. If you do not
mind my interfering, I would like to help you in your endeavour to
bring aid to these poor people."

The Princess was overjoyed. "Oh Father, that would be
wonderful."

In the months that followed the Sultan and the Princess distributed food and clothing to the poor. After a time the Sultan said, "This is not enough. I am concerned that we will make these people dependent on our welfare. We need to find ways to make them more self-sufficient."

The Sultan hired some of them to come and work at the palace tending the grounds and caring for the horses. He also gave over to them some land on the outskirts of the city where they established gardens and grew vegetables for sale in the marketplace. As the months went by they found there were fewer and fewer they had to lend succour to. More and more of those who had previously been poor became self-sufficient and took pride in their new independence.

Augustus had been involved in all these endeavours. With her growing interest in the poor, Naomi's self-obsession seemed to wither away.

After a day when they had gone into the city to distribute welfare and checked on the enterprises of the newly employed, Augustus and the Princess retired to the Palace. They went to the anteroom that had for so long been their meeting place and began their meditation practice. When they had completed their practice, Augustus said to the Princess, "You know My Lady, I think it is time that I took you to the special place that I have told you about for so long."

Naomi smiled a contented smile. "Augustus, you are a charlatan. You know that I have already entered the place. You know that the special place was always inside me awaiting my regaining of my personal composure, and when that happened I needed no one to help me enter there. And you were always right. The special place was never far away—it was always here once my self-obsession had waned. But I know I can not dwell here indefinitely. Occasionally I will forget the lessons and my depression may return. Even so I know it will not be like before and my being aware of it will hasten its passing. You have given me life skills that not only allow me to enter this special place but will hasten my return to it when I inevitably forget my true self."

"You are indeed an able student, Princess!

EPILOGUE

Listen to the Exhortation of the Dawn!
Look to this Day!
For it is Life, the very Life of Life.
In its brief course lie all the
Verities and Realities of your Existence.
The Bliss of Growth,
The Glory of Action,
The Splendor of Beauty;
For Yesterday is but a Dream,
And To-morrow is only a Vision;
But To-day well lived makes
Every Yesterday a Dream of Happiness,
And every Tomorrow a Vision of Hope.
Look well therefore to this Day!
Such is the Salutation of the Dawn!

Kalidasa

They sat together in their normal meeting room. Augustus and the Princess had been through their meditation practice and the Princess was playing on her flute. Unexpectedly, the Sultan walked in. Surprised the Princess stopped playing. "No, no, my dear—please continue," implored the Sultan.

He sat down alongside Augustus on a cushion. The Princess played for another fifteen or twenty minutes and then put down her flute.

"It is a joy to hear you play, Naomi. I am so glad you have taken up your music again," said the Sultan. He turned and looked at Augustus. "Naomi has told me that you are talking of leaving us."

Augustus nodded. "My work is done," he said. "I have performed the task you brought me here to do. Well at least I have done what I could!"

"And so you have," agreed the Sultan. "Will you not stay a little longer? I am sure there are many more of my subjects that you could help."

"Sire, you are wise. And you have wise people around you. Your Grand Vizier is one such person and Naomi herself has grown in wisdom. You have the capacity to help your people as much as I do."

The Sultan shook his head. "I doubt it, Augustus. I am not disparaging the wisdom of those around me—I value that very much—but you seem to see the world so much differently from us, and you bring a new approach that adds so much value."

Augustus responded, "It is a concern of mine that I do not create dependence. If I were to stay, you would continue to bring your problems to me. Whereas my ambition is to see you self-sufficient—able to solve your own problems."

The Sultan nodded. "That is a noble ambition. But tell me, if that is your ambition for us, what is your ambition for yourself?"

Augustus was taken aback. He was so used to others demanding of him that it was strange to have someone asking of his own needs.

The Sultan continued, "You have been so beneficial to us that I should like to repay you. I can not tell you how much you have benefited us. To see my daughter restored in this way is such a joy that I feel compelled to reward you. But then you are such a strange fellow I find it difficult to know what you would appreciate."

Augustus smiled. The Sultan continued. "I can offer you wealth and I can offer you status, but I know from our discussions these are of little import to you."

The Princess interjected, "Augustus, you have helped me so much there must be a way we can help you."

"Princess, I do not seek for your aid. There is nothing that could give me greater pleasure than seeing you engaging productively with the world again."

"And, Augustus there is nothing that would give me greater pleasure than seeing you pursue those things that are important to you."

"Then it should not surprise you, Naomi, that what is important to me is to understand humanity. I will not benefit from material gifts. These have little import to me. But if you can help me understand the human condition better, I would be forever grateful."

If the truth were to be told, Augustus put this position, not only because it was true, but because he believed the Sultan and the Princess could not deliver a solution to his demand and would therefore let him be. But he underestimated the resolve of the Princess. And she had remembered the discussion that he had had with her many months ago when she had asked him of his ambitions.

"I knew you would not accept money from us, Augustus. But would you accept an opportunity to study with renowned philosophers and experts that have made it their life to understand the human condition?"

"What do you mean Princess?"

"What I mean Augustus, is that I have provided a scholarship for you to study at the renowned university in the country of Maladania."

Augustus was overwhelmed. He knew very well about this university and was greatly attracted by the prospect of studying there."

"Oh Sultan, your daughter has provided me a boon that is difficult to resist."

"Then do not resist, Augustus! You have brought us happiness. We would be so pleased if we could give you something in return."

Naomi smiled. "Well my little Buddhist, would you like to engage with the academics from the university in Maladania?"

"It seems a way to learn more about the nature of humanity, Princess. Therefore I can not refuse. But I must thank you for your generosity and your insight. There is little else you could have offered me that I could have accepted."

"Then it is settled," smiled the Sultan. "We are overjoyed to be able to give you this opportunity. You have given us so much it is gratifying to have you accept our gift."

"It has been a pleasure your highness. My time with your daughter has been a great joy to me."

And so it was that Augustus made plans to set off to Maladania to study at the famed university. But before he went he sought out the Grand Vizier who had become his friend and confidante.

"Well Abdullah, I am soon to leave. I wanted to thank you for your assistance. Without your insights into the Princess and her father my work would have been much more difficult."

"I am sorry you are leaving, my little Buddhist friend. I have learnt much from you. Your work has exceeded my expectations. Not only have your restored the Princess but you have expanded the view of the Sultan as well. We will all benefit from that. And I understand the Princess has bestowed a scholarship on you. I am little surprised. She approached me about what might tempt you and I found it hard to respond."

Augustus smiled. "Well she did show some insight. But I recall a time when she asked me about my ambitions. I responded that I wished to understand the human condition better. Although I had no intention of influencing her to do anything about it, she has offered me an opportunity to do just that. And whilst I am grateful to the insights that my Buddhist teachings have provided, I am happy to learn from other traditions as well."

"I am pleased that she has provided you with this opportunity but I must say I am saddened to see you leave."

Augustus put his hand on Abdullah's shoulder. "You are a fine man my friend and, whilst I also have enjoyed your company, remember the dangers of attachment. You and I will go our separate ways. If fate wills it we will meet again and that would be good. If not I have pleasant memories that will ensure your kindness and wisdom will always abide with me."

"When do you leave us?" asked the Grand Vizier.

"In the morning," Augustus replied, "I set off for the port of Albazid and all going well, in three days time will set sail for Maladania."

The two friends chatted convivially for a while and then Augustus begged leave to retire.

In due course he made his way to Albazid and as per schedule set sail to Maladania. And there Augustus was to have another adventure. But that's another story!

AFTERWORD

In fact I have already written the story of the adventures of Augustus in Maladania. That tale began by saying he had been bestowed a scholarship by a Princess that he had helped cope with depression. When revising that manuscript I began to wonder about how that might have come about. That prompted me to write this book. I discovered this little story as a result!

I had initially put these words in the preface, but a good friend advised it was inappropriate to give that away at the very beginning of the story.

That seemed to make sense to me so I have now placed this explanation at the end.